*May the b*

Kimberly and I were alone in the hallway, staring each other down in front of the lockers.

Ever since she came back to Sweet Valley, I had tried to keep things with Kimberly friendly. But her running against me for student council president made it awfully hard. The whole club was divided. Still, maybe it was time for another try.

"Kimberly," I said in my nicest voice, "I don't really want to get into a big competition with you. Can't we work something out? Maybe we could be running mates or something."

Kimberly gave me a nasty smile. "Why, Mary, are you afraid to compete with me?"

"I'm not afraid," I said evenly. "I just don't like to see so many people get hurt. The Unicorns just got over a big fight, and now we're squaring off against each other again. The club doesn't need this."

"This *club*," Kimberly said with a sneer, "has turned into the biggest bunch of goody-goody geekoids I've ever seen. I think what you need is a little shaking up. A little competition. A little excitement."

A little trouble was what she meant.

Bantam Books in THE UNICORN CLUB series.
Ask your bookseller for the books you have missed.

*To Taryn Rebecca Adler*

# One

It was probably the liveliest Unicorn meeting we had ever had. I know it was the loudest.

We were all at the Wakefields' house on a Thursday afternoon, sitting in their big living room, clowning around and laughing.

Mandy Miller, our president, was sitting on the sofa in front of the coffee table, trying to get us all to be quiet and pay attention.

"Come on, you guys!" Mandy bellowed for about the fifth time. She pounded her green plastic gavel on the coffee table for emphasis, and it squeaked. (Actually, Mandy's gavel is a kid's squeaker toy. We got it for her as a

"How car            Unicorn meeting if you guys won't be q            attention?" she demanded.

            Jessica Wakefield, giggling.

"Lila and Ellen are making me laugh."

They *were* being pretty funny. But more than that, it was fun just being together again. I don't know if you heard about any of this, but not too long ago the Unicorns had a really big blowup. So big it broke up the club for a while.

See, a bunch of Unicorns suddenly found boyfriends. They had so much fun being part of a couple that they totally ignored the club. They were too busy to attend any Unicorn Club meetings or take part in any Unicorn activities.

I hate to admit this, but one of those girls was me.

Then Rick Hunter had the nerve to ask two girls to go with him to the same dance. He planned to stand one of the girls up.

I hate to admit this, but one of those girls was me. (Did I say that before? Ha ha!)

Well, the joke was on Rick. When the Unicorns found out about his plan, we were mad. So mad we forgot our differences and united against a common enemy: Rick Hunter.

We knew we had to let everyone know that we might have our disagreements, but we still cared about one another's feelings.

So we came up with a counterattack. Everybody was involved in a school play at the time. Some of us completely rewrote a scene Rick was in so that he made a complete fool of himself on stage in front of the whole school.

He got the message, all right. And so did everybody else. No way would somebody try to pull a two-faced trick like that on a Unicorn now.

Anyway, after that incident, the boyfriend thing sort of cooled down, and now we're all one big happy club again. And we decided not to carry a grudge against Rick. He learned his lesson, so we're all pretty good friends with him again. OK, so he's not number one on *my* list of favorite people, but for the most part I'm over him.

Now, some of us are old Unicorns. And some of us are new Unicorns. Let me explain:

The old Unicorns are people who were Unicorns last year. Like me. I'm Mary Wallace, and I'm in the eighth grade this year at Sweet Valley Middle School in Sweet Valley, California. I have long blond hair and I make really good grades. People tell me I'm pretty, but I think they say it to make me feel good. Personally, I think my nose is too big and my eyes are too close together. If I say that, though, everybody just laughs at me.

The other old Unicorns are Lila Fowler (who has the biggest wardrobe in Sweet Valley), Ellen Riteman, and Jessica Wakefield. Jessica's identical twin, Elizabeth, just joined this year. So that makes her a new Unicorn.

Elizabeth and Jessica Wakefield look exactly alike. Both girls have the same shoulder-length blond hair. The same blue-green eyes. And the same dimple in their left cheeks. But inside, they're as different as night and day.

How?

Just keep reading and you'll find out.

Last year, the Unicorn Club had a reputation for being mean and snobby. But this year Janet Howell, our old president, left middle school and went on to ninth grade at Sweet Valley High. So did Tamara Chase and Grace Oliver. Belinda Layton transferred to private school, and Kimberly Haver moved out of town to Atlanta.

Without them around we needed to regroup and pick a new president. But both Lila and Jessica wanted to run the Unicorns, so we ended up having a dare war. Talk about a disaster! We didn't solve any of our problems, and we got ourselves into major trouble.

Then Mandy Miller said we should be a club that brings out the best in its members—not the worst.

We liked that motto so much, we elected Mandy president. Her first official act was to make Maria Slater and Elizabeth Wakefield members. When the club had been in danger of being disbanded by the principal, Mr. Clark, it was Elizabeth (with Maria's help) who convinced him we had changed. So Mandy figured the least she could do was offer to make them members.

At first I wasn't sure they would accept. Elizabeth is a really good student, fair-minded and down to earth. Like I said, it's only on the outside that she and Jessica are the same. Jessica's smart, but she doesn't work very hard at school. She spends most of her time talking and giggling and flirting. Which is not to say the other Unicorns and I don't do our fair share of talking, giggling, and flirting. But Jessica has raised it to an art form.

Maria Slater has coffee-colored skin, is very tall, and used to be a child actress in Hollywood. Her family moved to Sweet Valley last year. Amy Sutton moved away over the summer, so I guess Maria is officially Elizabeth's best friend now.

Maria had doubts about us, just as Elizabeth did. But seeing us in action at the day-care center convinced them both that we had changed. We were sentenced to work at the day-care center as punishment for the dare war. But when our time was up, we all realized that we really loved the kids. So we stayed on. Now we all work there as volunteers on a regular basis.

Our last member is Evie. She's the youngest member, and she's in the sixth grade. She just moved to Sweet Valley from Hollywood with her grandmother, who's a retired actress.

So that's it. The whole Unicorn lineup. Now you know who we are and what we're all about, so back to the meeting. . . .

"Let's just adjourn so we can talk and eat cookies," suggested Evie.

"I second the motion. We've covered all the important stuff," Lila said with a smile. "All that's left is planning the party for the kids at the Center next week. And we can do that *and* eat cookies."

"We may need to postpone the party," Mandy said, thoughtfully tapping her gavel in the palm of her other hand.

Immediately, all the giggling died down, and the smiles gave way to looks of confusion.

"Postpone it?" Lila cried. "Why?"

"If we do that, the kids will be so disappointed," Elizabeth said.

There was a lot of muttering and arguing, but I could tell by Mandy's face that she had something important to announce.

Mandy whapped the gavel on the coffee table again.

*Squeak! Squeak!*

But this time nobody laughed.

"It's a shame to postpone the party for the kids," Mandy agreed. "But we've got a couple of items of new business, and one of them may wind up taking a lot of our time over the next couple of weeks."

New business?

I sat forward, eager to hear what Mandy was going to say. We don't usually have much new business at our meetings. Normally, we just read the minutes from the last meeting, talk for a few minutes, and adjourn.

*Whap!* went the gavel on the coffee table. *Squeak!*

"Please be quiet," Mandy said in her most presidential voice.

"Nobody was talking," Evie pointed out.

Mandy blushed. "I know. I guess I just like pounding my gavel."

Everybody laughed and applauded. We all knew how much it meant to Mandy to be president of the Unicorns. Last year, Mandy had cancer. She came through it, though. And she's all right now. But none of us will ever forget how scary and awful things were for a while.

Mandy cleared her throat. "Item number one on the agenda," Mandy read from her notes. "The student council elections are coming up. We're voting for president, vice-president, secretary, and treasurer. I think a Unicorn should run for president."

Maria raised her hand and was acknowledged. "Maria?"

"Aren't those things basically popularity contests?" she said. "I thought the Unicorns were into doing things that were more worthwhile."

"Like planning parties for the kids at the Center," Ellen Riteman said. "I don't think we should delay a party at the Center just because of some student election. Nobody pays any attention to stuff like that anyway."

"They do too!" Maria, Mandy, and I all shouted back.

(That's kind of a typical Ellenism. *She* doesn't pay any attention to things like student government, so she just assumes that everybody else feels the same way—which they don't.)

"Sorr*ee*," Ellen muttered, a blush creeping across her face.

Mandy waited a moment and then said tactfully, "Ellen's right. People really don't pay as much attention to council elections as they should. So they don't bother to run or campaign on any issues. Since there's no platform to vote on, people just vote for somebody they like. So it *does* become a popularity contest. But school government is just like national government. You get the government you deserve. If you don't participate, you can't complain about your government. So if one of us runs, we'll run on an issue, not just on our name."

Ellen's blush was gone. She was nodding really seriously, as if everything Mandy was saying was exactly what she had been trying to say all along. Which probably isn't true because . . . well . . . Ellen isn't stupid exactly, but she's no deep thinker either.

What Mandy was saying did make good sense, though. Student councils can do a lot for a school. They can collaborate with faculty to work out disciplinary measures that are fair. And they can take the students' complaints right to the principal.

I have a friend who goes to high school in another school district. She told me that her student council worked with the faculty at her school to get all the necessary money and equipment to make their bathrooms wheelchair-accessible.

Clearly, student councils could be effective—*if*

the people who served on them wanted them to be effective.

". . . nominate Mary."

Huh? Did I hear that right?

Unless my ears were deceiving me, someone had just nominated *me* to run for student council president.

"I second the nomination," Elizabeth Wakefield said quickly, her blue eyes glancing over at me. *Why not?* I thought, and nodded.

"All for it?" said Mandy.

"Aye!" everyone shouted.

Mandy whacked the coffee table with her plastic gavel.

*"Squeak!"*

"The ayes have it. The motion is carried. Mary is now officially a candidate for president of the Sweet Valley Middle School student council—at least as far as we're concerned. We'll still have to formally nominate her at the assembly on Tuesday."

Everyone jumped up and started crowding around me. Mandy stood up on the sofa and shouted, *"Guys! Guys! This is a meeting, and it's not over!"* Everyone ignored her. Then, since there was nothing nearby to pound her plastic gavel on, she squeezed it hard. *Squeak!*

"Order!" she thundered. "Order!" The whole time she kept on squeaking the toy gavel. *Squeak, squeak, squeak!*

She looked so serious and silly—scowling at us

and squeezing the gavel—it broke us up all over again. Finally, though, we pulled ourselves back together.

"Last item of business," Mandy said. "Kimberly Haver called me."

"From Atlanta?" Lila asked.

Mandy shook her head. "Nope. From right here. Her dad's gone to work for another company here in town, so they moved back."

Kimberly Haver was an old Unicorn whose father's company's corporate headquarters had moved from Sweet Valley to Atlanta. I had heard that the Havers weren't happy about the move. They had liked living in Sweet Valley, and both sets of Kimberly's grandparents were here. So even though they had only moved to Atlanta over the summer, Mr. Haver must have continued to try to find another job here, even if it meant working for a different company.

I guess that kind of shows you what a great place Sweet Valley is.

"As of Monday," Mandy continued, "Kimberly will be coming back to Sweet Valley Middle School."

Jessica, Ellen, and Lila all jumped up and screamed with excitement.

"Kimberly is *so cool*," Ellen crowed.

"Funny, too," Jessica added.

The next thing I knew, Jessica was urging everybody to stand and applaud.

I didn't join in right away. There was a millisec-ond-long pause while I tried to decide if this was good news or bad news.

Maria turned toward me. "I'm glad she's com-ing back," she said with a smile. "I didn't know Kimberly that well before. But my motto is, the more the merrier."

Elizabeth smiled. "Mine, too. It'll be fun getting to know her."

I wasn't a hundred percent sure that they were going to have fun getting to know Kimberly. But for the club's sake, I put on a big smile and joined in the applause. The whole time, though, my heart was sinking slowly down toward my shoes.

I did know Kimberly pretty well. And . . . well . . . she wasn't my favorite person in the world.

"Mary! Wait up!" I had just started walking home from the meeting when I heard someone call. I turned and saw Maria Slater running toward me.

She was breathless by the time she caught up with me. "You left so fast," she panted. "I was hop-ing we could walk home together." She elbowed me slyly. "Or don't budding politicians hobnob with ordinary mortals?"

I smiled thinly. It was the best I could manage.

Maria's smile disappeared. "What's the matter with you? I've heard about politicians who look old and harried when they leave office, but you look old and harried before you've even run."

That got a laugh out of me.

"If you're worried about the election, don't be," she said. "We'll all be behind you. You know that. And the club needs something like this. We've been through some bad times lately. I think we need something we can all work on together."

I nodded. "I know. I agree. But I wasn't thinking about the election."

"You weren't?"

I shook my head. "I was thinking about Kimberly Haver coming back."

Maria took my arm and pulled me toward the steps of a nearby building. "Sit down." I sat. "Now, talk to me."

I sighed. "Kimberly Haver is a really great person," I said. "She was—I mean *is*—a good Unicorn, but . . ."

"But you don't like her," Maria finished for me.

"No. I mean yes. I mean, I *do* like her . . . sometimes."

Maria didn't say anything judgmental or negative. She just looked at me. She was there to listen. And I was ready to talk. I'd never really confided my feelings about Kimberly to any of the other Unicorns. Everybody else adored Kimberly.

"She's so hip," I began. "And cool and flip and funny. She was a real Unicorn. Not like me. I always felt sort of like a fake Unicorn. I mean, I'm different—I take school pretty seriously and gossip isn't my best sport. Oh, I don't know what I'm trying to say. It sounds like I'm trying to say I'm better than she is, and that's not what I'm trying to say. But what I'm trying to say sounds worse."

"Say it anyway. It's just me. And if it's so horrible it makes me faint or run away, you can always deny you said it later."

"What?" I said, giggling.

"I'm teaching you how to think like a politician."

That made us both laugh. And when I looked over at Maria's face, it looked so open and friendly that I knew I could trust her. Maybe because she wasn't one of the old Unicorns.

I took a big breath. Then I closed my eyes and let it all come out. All the thoughts I'd had for so long but had been afraid to tell anyone.

"What I really think is that Kimberly is jealous of me on some level, because she's always competing with me. Grades. Boys. Clothes. Everything! And whatever we're competing over, she usually wins. I mean, when she puts her mind to it, she can always pull a better grade than I can. But she never seems to be interested in getting good grades unless I'm in her class. And if I have a new dress, Kimberly immediately goes out and buys two new dresses. If a guy talks to me, Kimberly will brag at lunch that he was flirting with her."

I stood up and waved my arms in irritation. "So if she's trying to prove she's better than I am, or smarter than I am, or prettier than I am, or more popular, she's done it already."

Maria nodded, and I could tell she understood what I was talking about.

"So why does she feel like she has to keep doing it all the time? It really gets on my nerves. And it makes me feel like I can never relax. Ever."

"Hold it. Hold it. Hold it," Maria said soothingly. "I don't blame you, but maybe you're getting a little carried away. What you're describing sounds totally obnoxious. But maybe Kimberly's changed over the summer."

I let out a little snort.

"It's possible," Maria insisted. "Look how much the Unicorns have changed since Kimberly left."

I folded my arms across my chest. "She's not going to like that one little bit," I mumbled.

Maria stood, dusted her hands on the seat of her pants, and then opened them wide and shrugged. "Well, like it or not, she's outnumbered," Maria said. "She'll either change along with the group or find another bunch of girls to hang out with. It's just that simple."

I stood, hoisted my backpack, and handed Maria hers.

Unfortunately, I didn't think it was going to be nearly as simple as Maria thought.

# Two

"I've talked to Alex Betner, Tom McKay, and Aaron Dallas," Elizabeth said breathlessly as she hurried up to join me, Evie, Lila, and Jessica.

It was the next day, Friday. We were all standing in the front hall outside the auditorium waiting for the last bell, which would announce morning assembly.

"They've all promised to vote for you," Elizabeth said.

"But my candidacy isn't even official yet," I protested. "I won't actually be nominated until Tuesday."

"Doesn't matter," Evie said. "We're spreading the word early. Having a Unicorn run for council president has really boosted student interest. Look around."

Students were milling about in every direction. The long hallway with its acoustical ceiling tiles and linoleum floor echoed with the buzz of a dozen conversations. If you stopped to listen, you could overhear words like *vote* and *campaign* and *strategy*.

"Who else is running?" I asked nervously.

"I've heard rumors that there are going to be at least six candidates," Evie reported with a giggle.

Jessica blew out her breath in surprise. "Usually the teachers have to beg somebody to run."

"The word around school," Elizabeth said, "is that it's going to boil down to you, Randy Mason, and Lois Waller."

"Then it's in the bag," Lila said, rolling her eyes. "Tell me somebody's going to vote for one of those two geeks when they could vote for a Unicorn. *Puul-ease.*"

"But that's not how I want to win," I cried. "I don't want to win a popularity contest. And stop calling them geeks!" I snapped. I saw everyone's face fall, and they began to back up a little.

"Sorry," Ellen muttered.

"Me, too," I said. "I shouldn't have yelled. But I hate it when you guys call people geeks."

As we filed into the auditorium for morning assembly, I started doing some serious thinking about why I had reacted so strongly.

If a good club was a club that brought out the best in its members, we were definitely on our way to becoming a terrible club. We weren't bringing out the best in one another. Not by a long shot.

Hearing Jessica and Lila sneer at Randy Mason

and Lois Waller just brought it all to the surface. Like how we almost disbanded permanently over something as silly as boyfriends. I had thought we really had changed, but maybe we really were the same Unicorns Janet Howell always used to push around. I hoped not.

"Is something bothering you?" Mandy asked me in a whisper. "It's not like you to be that touchy."

"I guess I'm afraid that when Kimberly gets back, we'll revert," I responded under my breath. "We'll turn back into the selfish, snotty club we were before."

"Hey!" Mandy cried in mock offense. "Don't forget, it's not exactly the same club anymore. Elizabeth is a member. Maria is a member. Evie is a member. And you and I are members. We outnumber the others."

I smiled at Mandy and Mandy smiled back. "We'll bring Kimberly up to speed on the new Unicorns. No problem," Mandy whispered in a confident voice.

Then the people behind us started shushing us, because Mr. Clark was stepping up to the podium.

He cleared his throat, and the audience became silent.

"As you all know, there's a lot of construction work being done in the school cafeteria. As a result, we've been forced to close off big sections of the seating area and allow some students to leave campus for lunch."

This was old news. Since the cafeteria couldn't accommodate as many people as before, the school had tried something experimental. They had let the seventh- and eighth-grade kids leave campus for lunch.

There's a four-block shopping area across the boulevard behind the school. It's got tons of places to eat and shop. A pizza place. A burger joint. An ice cream place. A comic book shop. A video arcade. A shoe store. You name it, and it's there.

Being able to leave campus has been a total blast. It's made us all feel like we're in college—or at least high school.

Mr. Clark cleared his throat again. "I'm sure you have all noticed the construction also being done behind the school."

People began shifting in their seats. What was he getting at? You couldn't miss the construction project that was going on back there. It was huge. I mean, jillions of trucks and cement mixers and hard-hatted men.

"The traffic has to use a single-lane detour, making it hard to safely cross the street there. Yesterday at lunchtime, a seventh-grade boy was struck by a car."

The whole assembly gasped.

Mr. Clark held up his hand, telling us not to panic. "The boy is fine. He's badly bruised, but miraculously, no bones were broken. But this accident has made us aware of how dangerous it is to have great numbers of students crossing that boulevard every day."

"Uh-oh," I heard a voice behind me groan. "I think I know where this is going."

"As a result of this incident, the faculty, school board, and PTA have agreed that the off-campus lunch privilege must be suspended until the road project is finished."

"No way!" Aaron Dallas blurted out.

An angry buzz immediately filled the auditorium.

Mr. Clark held up his hands for quiet, and after a few seconds the auditorium quieted down.

"I'm afraid it's simply unavoidable," Mr. Clark said.

"But you're treating us like morons," Rick Hunter complained.

"Please raise your hand if you have a remark to make, Rick," Mr. Clark said frostily.

Rick raised his hand, and Mr. Clark rolled his eyes and then pointed to him.

Rick stood. "You're treating us like morons," he repeated in a calmer, more dignified voice. "Like we're too dumb to look both ways before we cross."

Everybody in the auditorium was upset and mad. Everybody except the sixth graders. It didn't affect them.

"It's not forever," Mr. Clark reminded us. "It's only until the road construction is complete. And if you recall, we have made it clear from the beginning that leaving campus was a provisional privilege."

Elizabeth Wakefield raised her hand.

"Elizabeth?" Mr. Clark nodded in her direction.

Elizabeth stood. "I read in the newspaper that the road construction could take up to fifteen months to complete. That means we'll never get our privilege back this year."

Mr. Clark sighed. "I'm sorry. I know you're disappointed. But the faculty and the PTA are both adamant. There's simply too much risk involved. We'll have some picnic tables set up on the grounds out back to accommodate the overflow in the cafeteria. That is all."

Mr. Clark abruptly left the stage, which is his way of saying "That's that."

Everybody sat quietly in their seats for a few seconds, like they were still stunned. Then, slowly, they began to get up and leave. There was a lot of grumbling and mumbling all around me.

"I feel like somebody just canceled Christmas," Aaron Dallas said with a groan.

"The only thing I like about school is the off-campus lunch privilege," a seventh-grade girl said.

I felt like grumbling and mumbling myself. Leaving campus at lunch had been so cool.

We didn't all leave every day. Some of us always stayed on campus to eat with Evie so she wouldn't be left by herself. But still, we'd all done it often enough to get used to it.

Outside the auditorium, all the Unicorns gathered. Evie looked really sympathetic. "Gee. I know it doesn't affect me, but I'm sorry for you guys."

Ellen shrugged and kicked her toe against the floor. "We should have known that Mr. Clark would pull something like this."

"What do you mean?" Elizabeth asked.

"He's such a killjoy. Anything that's fun, he finds a way to put a stop to."

That wasn't really accurate. All things considered, Mr. Clark was a pretty good principal. But I could see Ellen's point. This did seem unbelievably unfair.

Maria sighed heavily. "What a blow! I liked being able to shop during lunch."

"And I liked being able to browse through the bookstore," Elizabeth mourned.

"Well, no sense standing around moaning about what we can't change," Mandy said briskly. "I'm going to class."

*Ring!*

There went the first bell. That meant we had five minutes to get to our lockers, get our books, and get to class.

We all exchanged a lot of listless good-byes, and then Elizabeth, Maria, Mandy, Evie, and I hurried off in one direction. And Jessica, Ellen, and Lila hurried off in another.

Looking back, I see it as sort of an omen of what was about to happen.

In the meantime, I had the upcoming nominations to think about.

In spite of the fact that I thought Lila's remark about Randy and Lois was way out of line, she did have a point. Randy was sixth-grade class president last year. He did a good job, but he wasn't very well known by the other classes.

And as for Lois . . . well, she's really really nice, but she doesn't make very good grades and she doesn't seem like a person with a lot of leadership ability. And she's way overweight. Not that something like that should matter. But a lot of kids don't take her very seriously because of her weight.

Maybe the election really was in the bag.

On the other hand, I remembered studying in my history class how everybody was sure that Thomas E. Dewey was going to win the presidential race of 1948. They were so sure that he was going to win that the newspaper went ahead and printed a headline that read DEWEY DEFEATS TRUMAN before the ballots were all counted.

But surprise, surprise. He didn't win. When all the votes were counted, Harry S. Truman was the winner.

I couldn't help thinking that if it came down to a matter of popularity, I was sure to win.

But I was serious about not wanting to win that way. And I didn't want to take anything for granted.

I was going to campaign seriously. And if I won, I'd know it was because I had taken a position that earned the confidence and trust of the Sweet Valley Middle School students.

Does that sound really dorky?

# Three

"Kimberly will flip when she sees that," Jessica said, giggling.

She was pointing toward Lila, who was sitting in a rocker reading to little Ellie McMillan from a book of fairy tales.

Jessica was right about Kimberly. Quietly reading to Ellie was not typical Lila Fowler behavior—or at least not like the Lila Fowler that Kimberly knew. In the old days, Lila Fowler hadn't had two minutes for anybody she didn't think was rich, popular, or stylish.

Ellie and her mom weren't rich or stylish. But Ellie was a little doll. She adored Lila and vice versa. In fact, one time when Ellie was upset, she ran away from home. And guess whose house she ran to? That's right. Lila's.

It was late Friday afternoon, and for once all of us were at the day-care center. Usually, we didn't all volunteer on the same day. But since we had had to postpone the party for the children, we thought it would be nice if we all came together for a couple of afternoons. That way we could entertain them. And party or no party, they'd still know they were important to us.

In fact, over the last several weeks most of us had developed a kind of big-sister relationship with one or more of the kids.

Jessica's favorite was Oliver Washington. If he wasn't a boy, four years old, and black, you'd think *he* was Jessica's twin. When Jessica and Oliver get together, they argue so loudly that sparks fly. But it's all forgotten a minute later, and everybody knows they're crazy about each other.

Arthur Foo is sort of like Ellen Riteman's foster brother. Arthur is a quiet Korean boy with a big family. Ellen has managed to really draw Arthur out over the last few weeks. He used to be quiet as a mouse. But Ellen's gotten him to participate in more games and activities.

Elizabeth and I always team up to keep an eye on Allison and Sandy Meyer. Wow! Talk about a pair of wild ones. You have to watch those two every minute. They're like some kind of Murphy's Law come to life: if there's any kind of trouble to get into, they'll find it.

Yuky Park is Asian and very quiet, but she always has a smile on her face. Especially when Mandy's around.

There are a lot of other children who come and go. And usually, we have a few toddlers.

The Center was full today, so it was a good thing we were all there.

"Mary!"

When I heard my name, I looked up and saw Mrs. Willard standing at the door. Mrs. Willard is the director of the Center. There's a small paid staff, but mostly the place is run by volunteers—us.

Mrs. Willard stood in the doorway and motioned for me to come over.

I threw some blocks back into the toy box and went over to see what she wanted.

"I just wanted to tell you girls how much it means to the children for all of you to come at once," she said. "They were so disappointed over the cancellation of the party, but having all of you here makes up for a lot."

Her face looked sad for a moment. "Some of these kids have had a lot of promises broken."

She was right. Most of the kids are from poor homes, and lots of them have single parents. Very few have the money for new toys and clothes and games and all the other stuff that most of us take for granted.

I say "most of us" because I was a foster child for a long time. I lived with a lot of different families until my real mom found me and made a home for the two of us. Then she married Tim, my stepfather, and he adopted me. So now we're like a real family. But I'll never forget those early years, or how much broken promises hurt.

Just then, Allison came running over to me with Sandy hard on her heels.

"Hug," Allison demanded, reaching her arms up.

I picked her up immediately and squeezed her hard. When I was a little girl, I don't think anybody ever hugged me. So when Sandy demanded a hug, too, I managed to hoist them both up and squeeze them until they began to laugh and wriggle out of my arms.

Mrs. Willard smiled again at me. "You girls are wonderful with the kids. Thanks again."

"I'm just sorry we have to postpone their party," I said.

Mrs. Willard shook her head and held up her hands, to tell me not to worry. "Elizabeth told me about the student council elections. That's every bit as important as what you do here. And I wish you the best of luck."

"Thanks, Mrs. Willard."

Mrs. Willard nodded briskly and put her hand on the swinging doors that separated the playroom from the hallway. "I'll be in my office. Call me if you need any help."

"I will," I promised.

After she left, Jessica came over, and I saw Lila put Ellie down by the playhouse.

"What's up?" Lila asked. "What did Mrs. Willard say?"

"Just that the kids really depend on us," I answered.

Jessica nodded. "Like I said, Kimberly's going to faint when she sees this. Can you imagine the old club volunteering for anything?"

Lila laughed. "Or anybody depending on us for anything?"

"I can't believe how selfish we were," Jessica said.

Lila shrugged. "Yeah. But we had a lot of fun, too. Remember the Valentine's Day dance?"

I cracked up and so did Mandy. Maria hadn't lived here then, so Mandy explained. "I'll never forget it. A couple of us helped Amy Sutton get dressed up like a hippie to impress Ken Matthews," Mandy wheezed. "She looked so hilarious."

"And remember the time we all had to do that marriage experiment and how silly and funny everybody began to act?"

Everybody was laughing now. We had had some great times last year.

Jessica smiled. "Remember the time you changed the lock on Randy Mason's locker right before the open-book English test?"

*Poof!* My good mood suddenly evaporated. I didn't like remembering stuff like that.

Lila threw back her head and laughed. "It was like watching Donald Duck. He went totally ballistic. Talk about crazed."

Jessica snickered meanly and began talking in a Donald Duck voice, supposedly imitating Randy. "Get a locksmith. Get the janitor. Get me an English book, quick."

"Too bad he found out it was us," Lila said.

Jessica rolled her eyes. "Tell me about it. Mr. Bowman gave us four hours of detention."

"Of course, we did put that lizard in his drawer."

Jessica couldn't stop laughing. "Made him jump ten feet."

"And turn about eight shades of red," Lila added.

"Like his face isn't red enough already. Remember when we used to call him Mr. Tomato Head?"

They both broke up, and that's when Ellen came over to join us. "What's so funny over here?"

"Just talking about the good old days. Remember when we put the lizard in Mr. Bowman's desk and locked Randy Mason out of his locker?" Jessica answered.

*Good old days?* Did Jessica really think of those old exploits as "the good old days"?

I felt my smile fade away as Ellen nodded and began talking about some mean trick they had played on Lois Waller last year.

Pretty soon all three girls were laughing.

They seemed to be having a good time reminiscing about the old days. *Too* good a time.

Sure, it was great being popular and exclusive,

and it was even sometimes fun getting into trouble together. But it wasn't great being snobby and mean. It was childish, and it hurt people's feelings.

Was Kimberly going to expect us to be the same old Unicorns? Gossipy? In trouble all the time? Mean-spirited?

I couldn't shake the feeling that I really didn't want Kimberly to come back. That what we had now was something special. And somehow, she was going to ruin things for us.

"Hey!" Ellen cried sharply.

I looked over and saw that quiet Arthur Foo was teamed up with Oliver Washington, and they were pelting Sandy and Allison with pieces of a jigsaw puzzle.

Ellen and Jessica took about six long steps in their direction and very quickly and efficiently broke up the fight.

"Come on, Arthur," Ellen coaxed, "let's go see what we can build with the blocks."

"Oliver," Jessica said, "would you do me a really big favor and hold this notebook for me?" Jessica pulled a notebook down off of a pile of papers on a shelf. "It's got some really important information in it about making desserts. See if you can find a picture of one we can make here." The playroom had a little kitchenette with a range and a fridge.

The funny feeling in my stomach began to ease up a little bit. Ellen and Jessica both looked kind and interested and generous. Nothing like their old Unicorn image.

I darted my eyes around the room, looking at each girl. All of this came naturally to the new Unicorns—Maria, Elizabeth, and Evie.

I felt perfectly comfortable with our new image, and I was beginning to think that Ellen and Jessica did, too.

Lila?

I wasn't sure. Lila blows so hot and cold, she's hard to read sometimes.

Later that afternoon, I went into the kitchen to make hot chocolate. Evie and Jessica were already there fixing snacks for the kids. "Ready for Tuesday?" Evie asked, interrupting my thoughts.

"Ready as I'll ever be," I said with a smile.

I still hadn't figured out what issues I would run on, but I had plenty of time. I turned to Jessica and Evie and said, "Want to come over this weekend and help me get an early start on my campaign strategy?"

Jessica smiled. "Sorry, I can't. Kimberly Haver's family is all unpacked and moved into their new house. She called last night and invited me to spend the night. In fact, she wants to have a slumber party for anybody who can make it on short notice."

"I can come," Lila said, joining us. She asked Ellen and Mandy.

Mandy called across the room, "Sure, I can go."

"Count me out," Ellen said mournfully. "I have to go with my folks to visit my grandmother."

"Better count me out, too," I said. "Aside from homework, I've got to think about my campaign. I'll have to wait until Monday to see Kimberly."

Nobody bothered to check with Elizabeth, Maria, or Evie (which I thought was kind of rude). But on the other hand, none of those girls had been Kimberly's friends in the past, so I guess it was logical not to ask them.

Still, it bothered me.

# Four

I didn't have a chance to talk to anybody over the weekend. Turned out my mom had about a jillion errands she needed me to do on Saturday. Just when I thought I'd finished everything, she handed me the grocery list.

"Mom," I protested as she took the list back and added a few items to it. "I really need some time to think about my campaign."

My mom laughed. "Campaign or no campaign, we have to eat next week. That means somebody's got to go to the grocery, and it can't be me because I've got to get to the dry cleaner before they close.

I sighed, took the list, got my jacket, and headed out. *Again!*

I love my mom, but sometimes I think she forgets I'm a kid.

\*        \*        \*

Saturday night I did homework. And on Sunday, I tried to think of some really hot issue that would get the students of Sweet Valley High all fired up to participate in the student council elections.

Of course, the hottest issue was the off-campus lunch privilege. Kids were mad the privilege had been revoked, and I didn't blame them. It wasn't any big deal to get across the street safely. Then I had an idea. What if I put together a petition that all the kids could sign saying they wanted their off-campus privilege back? But Mr. Clark had seemed to have his mind made up, so that was probably a waste of time.

I tried to think up some other issues, but I didn't come up with anything too exciting. But I wasn't worried. Once Elizabeth and I started brainstorming, I knew we'd come up with something.

So when I got to school on Monday, I hadn't talked to Jessica or Lila or heard anything about Kimberly.

Even though I knew she was coming back, it was still kind of a shock to see her standing on the front steps of the school with Jessica, Lila, and Ellen. Real déjà vu stuff. It was like a time warp. We were all a year younger, waiting on the front steps for Janet Howell, our old president.

Kimberly let out a squeal when she saw me, and I ran up and gave her a hug.

"I am *so* happy to be back. You wouldn't believe," she said.

"I'm glad you're back, too," I said, smiling at her.

She looked the same, only her dark hair was longer. Way past her shoulders.

"Your hair looks really pretty," I commented.

"It's longer than yours now," Kimberly immediately said.

I felt a little flicker of irritation. So her hair was longer. Big deal. From her tone, you would have thought she had just defeated me in the national gymnastics championships or something.

As usual, her clothes were really hip. She had on a short flared rayon skirt and a matching blouse. Next to Lila, Kimberly was always the biggest clothes horse in the bunch.

Then I noticed the purple satin jacket under her arm. It said *Unicorns* across the back in white script, just like ours. (We'd gotten them from Tom Sanders, the director of *Secondhand Rose*, a movie that had been shot at our school a while back.) "How did you get a jacket?" I asked in an amazed voice.

"I had my father's tailor copy mine," Lila said proudly. "And I paid him double his usual rate to have it ready in time for today." Lila smiled. "It was my way of saying welcome back."

Just then, Elizabeth and Evie came up the stairs together.

"Hi," Elizabeth called out in a really friendly tone.

She introduced Evie, and Kimberly said hello.

Then there was an awkward silence.

"So," Elizabeth chirped. "I guess you know Maria and Evie and I are Unicorns now."

"So I hear," Kimberly responded.

I don't know if it was my imagination, but I thought I heard a slightly sneery note in her voice.

Nobody seemed to hear it but me. Or if they did, they pretended not to.

"That's a pretty bracelet," Jessica commented.

"Thanks," Kimberly said. "This guy in Atlanta gave it to me over the summer."

Of course, anything having to do with boys got everybody's attention. Kimberly went on to tell us about what a great summer she had had with a bunch of guys she had gotten to know in Atlanta. She said she had told them about the Unicorns— how pretty and popular we were.

Then she gave us the big finish: she said the guys all wanted to come to Sweet Valley next summer to meet us.

Needless to say, all of us wanted to hear more. Everybody was asking Kimberly questions at once: Had she been out on any "real" dates? Were the guys cute? Were they older? How many guys would come?

It was like Kimberly Haver had just become the most glamorous person in Sweet Valley.

"The guys are prime-time cute," Kimberly promised.

Then, suddenly, I had this weird thought. I

began to wonder if she was even telling the truth. Kimberly Haver had been known to stretch the truth a little from time to time.

But just as that thought was crossing my mind, Lila piped in with, "She's not kidding. Jessica and I saw a bunch of photographs when we spent the night on Saturday. You can't believe how cute the guys are."

*Ring!*

It was the second bell, which meant we all had to rush to class—pronto.

"I'll tell you more at lunch," Kimberly promised as we went inside the building. "See you at the Unicorner," she called over her shoulder as she hurried toward the stairwell.

At lunchtime, we were all at the Unicorner (which is what we call the table where we always sit) when Kimberly came over with her tray. Sarah Thomas and Sophia Rizzo were sitting with us, too. And of course, Elizabeth, Maria, and Evie.

Kimberly looked startled to see so many people. "Well, this is certainly a change," she said in a sugary-sweet voice. "Are Sarah and Sophia Unicorns now, too?"

Elizabeth smiled. "No," she said, "but the new Unicorns enjoy doing things with different people."

There was a long, uncomfortable pause while everybody waited for Kimberly's reaction.

Finally, she smiled. "Great," she said.

Sarah and Sophia looked really uncomfortable. "Maybe we should sit someplace else," Sophia whispered to me.

She started to rise, but involuntarily, I shot my hand out and took her wrist. "No!" I insisted. "Stay!"

Sophia looked uncertainly from face to face. Evie, Maria, Elizabeth, and Mandy all smiled encouragingly.

But Jessica's and Lila's faces were neutral. And Ellen actually had a frown on her face.

Oh, boy! They didn't look as though they were definitely on Kimberly's side. But they weren't going out of their way to put Sarah and Sophia at ease, either.

Kimberly didn't say anything more about Sarah and Sophia sitting with us. But she very pointedly sat down as far from them as possible—so that she was way over to the left, next to Ellen and Lila and across from Jessica.

"We were just talking about the day-care center," Elizabeth said to Kimberly. "Sarah and Sophia might want to do some volunteer work there. You, too, if you want."

"No, thanks," Kimberly said abruptly. "I don't like messing around with little kids."

"It's more fun than you think," Jessica said. "We made these puppets for their last party and—"

"Puppets!" Kimberly exclaimed in a really sarcastic tone, interrupting Jessica. "How exciting," she drawled.

Her voice was so contemptuous that Jessica turned pale and Ellen turned red. Lila's face went blank, and Mandy snapped back slightly, as if she had been slapped.

Maria tugged lightly on my sleeve. "I think maybe the old Unicorns need to clue Kimberly in on the new Unicorn philosophy alone," she whispered.

I nodded. "I think you're right. And I'm really sorry," I added miserably.

The whole situation was making me feel so embarrassed. Kimberly was a perfect example of what the Unicorns used to be like. And it wasn't a pretty picture.

"Hey! Don't sweat it," Maria said with a reassuring smile. Then she looked at Elizabeth, Evie, Sophia, and Sarah and gave a slight jerk of her head. They all picked up their trays and made excuses about having to get to the library before class.

I looked across the table at Mandy. She was furiously spinning her spaghetti around on her fork, trying to act as if she hadn't been paying attention to what was going on. But I knew she had been paying attention, because her face was beet red.

Kimberly smiled and watched them leave. Then, as soon as they were out of earshot, she looked at us and shook her head. "I don't believe you guys. What a bunch of goody-goodies. Baby-sitting!" she huffed. "Puppet shows! What would Janet Howell say?"

"We don't care what Janet Howell would say!" I

retorted hotly. Then I stopped myself. Yelling at her wouldn't make Kimberly agree with me.

I took a deep breath and forced my voice to sound friendly and welcoming. "Look. The old Unicorn Club was great. But the new Unicorn Club is better. We accomplish things. We're useful. We're—"

"—goody-goodies," Kimberly finished for me.

I swallowed the anger that was rising in my throat and looked desperately around the table for help. But nobody said anything. I couldn't believe it. What a bunch of cowards.

But then Mandy spoke up. "Kimberly," she said softly, "we're all really glad you're back. But the club has changed. We've had our differences and our troubles, but basically, we're glad we're not the way we used to be. Give it a chance, OK?"

Kimberly's face relaxed and she smiled. Not that tight, sarcastic smile. But a real smile. (Mandy has a real way with people. She wants to be a clothing or costume designer when she grows up. But I think she should be a diplomat.)

"OK, OK," Kimberly said in a bored tone. She took a big sip of her milk and put down the container. "So tell me more about these, um, puppets."

Mandy launched into an enthusiastic description of the puppets we had made and how much the kids had laughed and applauded when we put on a puppet show.

But as soon as Mandy was finished, Kimberly started asking about who had crushes on whom.

Who was dating whom. And what Janet thought about high school.

Soon, Kimberly had us all laughing and giggling and gossiping. A wave of nostalgia washed over me. This was how it used to be. This was the part of the old Unicorn Club that I missed. The inside jokes that only we could understand. The way Kimberly could always say "Cool" in this fake California surfer accent and break us all up.

I remembered the sense of belonging I used to feel. When I looked at the faces around the table, it almost gave me goose bumps. Kimberly, Ellen, Jessica, and Lila seemed to belong to one another.

*I belong, too,* I reminded myself.

Or did I?

The next day was Tuesday. The big day. I had butterflies in my stomach as I waited outside the auditorium.

People were pushing past me on their way in. But I held my ground even though it was hard not to get swept along. I was waiting for the rest of the Unicorns. We had all planned to sit together during this assembly.

Elizabeth arrived first. "Nervous?"

I shook my head. "Not really."

She smiled. "Good. Nothing to be nervous about today. All we're doing is nominating people. And it's all set. I'll nominate you and Maria will second the motion."

I nodded. We'd been over all this two or three
times already.

Finally, I saw Kimberly coming down the hall
flanked by Jessica and Lila. Ellen trailed behind
them.

There was something jittery about Ellen. And
Jessica had her mouth held tight in this little half
smile she gets when she's up to something.

Before I could wonder what was going on, Evie
appeared. Mandy materialized at my elbow. And
Maria came running around the corner with her
backpack banging against her arm. "All right!" she
said. "All present and accounted for. Let's go in
there and do it."

We all high-fived and then made our way into
the auditorium.

All around us, people were talking and laughing
and pushing, but we finally found a row of seats
where we could all sit together.

I wound up sitting next to Kimberly.

After everybody got seated and settled, Mr. Clark
stepped up on the stage, went to the podium, and
then made some long and boring speech about the
importance of student government. Blah blah blah.

I squirmed a little in my seat. For some reason, I
really was nervous. I wished Mr. Clark would
hurry up and get to the nominations.

Finally, the moment we had all been waiting for
arrived.

As predicted, Peter DeHaven nominated Randy

Mason, and Rick Hunter seconded the motion.

Cammi Adams nominated Lois Waller.

Mr. Clark asked if anyone would second the motion. Not one hand went up. Ugghhhh. It was just awful. And how embarrassing for Lois.

"Will anyone second the motion?" Mr. Clark repeated.

Nobody made a move.

I couldn't stand it. I just couldn't stand to see Lois humiliated that way. Before I knew it, my hand shot up. "I second the motion," I said.

Everybody kind of buzzed and murmured, but there were also a few sighs of relief.

Elizabeth gave me a wink and a nod. And when I looked behind me, I saw Lois smile gratefully.

"Any other nominations?" Mr. Clark asked.

Elizabeth raised her hand. "I nominate Mary Wallace," she said in a firm voice.

"I second the motion," Maria said immediately.

Mr. Clark wrote my name down on his list, and then he took off his glasses, which meant that he thought the assembly was pretty much over.

"Any other nominations?" he mumbled, looking as if he really didn't expect any.

Much to his surprise—and mine—Jessica stood up. "I nominate Kimberly Haver," she said in a voice that seemed to ring out through the auditorium.

I heard Maria suck in her breath with a surprised gasp, and Elizabeth's head snapped to the left to see what in the world was going on.

"I second the motion," Lila said, rising and standing beside Jessica.

Mr. Clark looked really surprised, but he put his glasses back on and wrote Kimberly's name on his list.

"Any other nominations?" he asked.

There was nothing but silence from the audience. He went on to take nominations for vice-president and the other offices.

"All right, then. The election will take place a week from Thursday. Between now and then, I advise each candidate to do their best to come up with a specific platform and to campaign before and after school. On Election Day, you will hear final speeches from the candidates and then cast your vote at the end of that assembly."

I couldn't believe it. I was numb with shock. What was going on? When had Kimberly Haver decided to run? And why had Jessica and Lila agreed to nominate her? How could they do something like this without discussing it with me first?

My mind was still whirring and racing as Mr. Clark dismissed the assembly and everybody started filing out. Out of the corner of my eye, I saw Mandy hurry past the row of kids that separated her from the aisle and disappear out of the auditorium.

Finally, I found my tongue and turned toward Kimberly. "What are you trying to do?" I demanded angrily. Then I looked past her at Ellen, Jessica, and Lila. "And you guys! I can't believe you knew about this and didn't tell me!"

Ellen and Jessica at least looked ashamed. Their faces were pointed down at the floor and they were silent.

"Gosh, Mary," Lila said in her most innocent voice, "I thought you of all people would understand. Kimberly just wants to feel like she's involved. It's hard, starting in the middle of the term and all."

"I just wanted to participate in a school activity," Kimberly added sweetly.

It was the same old thing. Kimberly was determined to compete with me. *I* was running for president of the student council, so *she* had to run, too. Well, she could just forget it.

I stood up and yanked my book bag off the floor. "I'm not going to play this game with you," I said angrily. "If you're determined to run, fine. I'll drop out."

"Uh, Mary," Maria said in my ear.

But I couldn't stop myself. "Then *you* can run against Randy and Lois. But P.S.: don't count on my vote."

"Mary," Maria repeated more urgently. "Can I talk to you? *Now!*"

I could feel the anger boiling over inside me. I couldn't believe that my friends would betray me like this.

Finally Maria pulled me over to one side, and Elizabeth came with her.

"You have to run," Maria said in a whisper.

Elizabeth nodded. "You do. Don't you see?

Kimberly is just trying to stir up trouble. She wants the Unicorn Club back the way it was. Somehow she's gotten Ellen and Jessica and Lila to go along with her on this. I don't know about Mandy."

Her eyes hardened. "We can't let them think we're going to roll over and play dead. The Unicorns need you. You've got to rise to this challenge. Don't surrender to the troublemaker. If you do, she'll take over the Unicorns and force you and me and Maria and Evie out."

Elizabeth was right. Kimberly Haver had always been a troublemaker. In fact, some of us used to call her the Spoon, because she was always stirring things up. Like telling me that Jessica had said something mean about me. Then when I would get mad at Jessica, she wouldn't know why, and that would make her mad with me. We could spend days angry at each other—all because of Kimberly.

Why did we put up with it? I'm not sure, except that Kimberly always had a reputation for being cool and hip and full of gossip and inside information on people, places, and things. And she wasn't afraid of Janet Howell, either. She never let Janet push her around. Which made her seem more grown up than the rest of us.

"It's not just the election that's at stake," Elizabeth said. "It's the future of the Unicorns."

Maria nodded her head.

On the other side of the hall, Kimberly and the others were laughing and talking. Every so often, they would snicker as someone passed—making it obvious that they were laughing at them.

This made me furious. How could they behave that way? And also, did I want someone like Kimberly representing the Unicorn Club on the council?

No way.

I wanted somebody with good character. Somebody sensitive. Somebody who really cared about accomplishing good things at school.

In other words, me.

I know it sounds conceited, but that's the way I felt.

I straightened my shoulders and took a deep breath. "Come with me," I said to Maria, Elizabeth, and Evie.

They were a little confused, but they followed me over to where Kimberly and the others stood.

"Look, Kimberly, it would be better all around if there were only one Unicorn in the race. But I'm not dropping out, and if you want to run, that's your right. I just think we should all try to keep the competition friendly."

"I agree one hundred percent," Kimberly said.

"Fair fight?" I asked tentatively.

"Fair fight," Kimberly agreed.

Everybody shook hands all around, and Maria smiled. "OK, then. Everybody run a good clean race, and may the best Unicorn win."

# Five

I found Mandy after third period. Her locker was near mine, and I went over to her while she was getting some of her books out.

When she turned and saw me, it was almost as though she was embarrassed. Her cheeks turned pink, and she had a hard time looking me in the eye.

"Did you know what Kimberly was planning?" I asked.

Mandy shook her head. "No. I didn't," she said in an expressionless voice.

There was a long pause, and for the first time in my life, I felt like grabbing Mandy by the shoulders and shaking her. "Don't you have anything to say about it?" I demanded.

That got a reaction. Mandy shut her locker with an angry bang. "No. As a matter of fact, I don't."

"Well, you should," I said, feeling angrier by the minute. "You're supposed to be our president."

Mandy took a deep breath, then another. She looked as if she was trying not to get upset. "I know," she said finally. "But I'm your friend, and I'm Kimberly's friend. I just can't take a side, Mary. I wish Kimberly hadn't done this. But I can't stop her. And I can't officially support you or her."

"But you know how Kimberly is," I protested. "She's everything we've worked hard not to be anymore. Snobby. Superficial. Exclusive. And she's turning Lila and Jessica and Ellen into carbon copies of herself."

Mandy looked up at the ceiling, then back down, and let out a huge sigh. "I know. But I also know that when I had cancer last year and felt so sick from the medication, Kimberly came over and read to me every afternoon. She also kept duplicate notes in history so I could stay current with the class. And when Mom and I moved into our new house and were so broke, Kimberly came over and helped us paint our dining room."

Mandy's eyes met mine squarely. "I also remember your coming by the house every afternoon with fresh-baked cookies and new library books for me and . . ."

"Oh, Mary," Mandy said. "I don't know what to do. I just don't know. Both of you are great friends. And I feel like you're breaking my heart in two."

I closed my eyes and concentrated really hard. I

tried to put myself in Mandy's shoes. And I began to feel what she was feeling. To think what she was thinking.

To me, the choice was clear. I couldn't believe anybody would choose Kimberly over me.

But to Mandy, Kimberly had been a devoted and unselfish friend.

I put my arm around Mandy's shoulder. "It's OK. You don't have to take a side. In fact, it probably wouldn't be ethical if you did."

Mandy's eyes flew up and met mine. They shone with hope. "What do you mean?"

"I mean that as president of the Unicorns, you have a duty to remain impartial."

Mandy's face had gone white, but now she began to get a little color back. "You mean you won't be angry if I don't work on your campaign?"

"Just so long as you don't work on Kimberly's either," I said. "Your job is not to campaign but to make sure it's a fair race between us and to keep the club together."

Mandy bit her lower lip, as if she was thinking it over. After a minute, she made a rueful face. "You're right. But I'm just so afraid this is going to turn ugly."

"You can count on me to keep it clean," I promised.

"Am I interrupting a closed-door meeting?" joked a voice from behind us.

We both whirled around and saw Kimberly Haver standing there.

"We were just talking about the race," I said, trying to make my voice sound friendly.

Kimberly nodded. "What did you decide?"

Mandy swallowed. "I'm not going to take a side," she blurted out. I could tell it took her a lot of courage to say it.

"I think that's the only fair course of action for Mandy," I said. In spite of my efforts to sound calm, there was a little note of defiance in my voice.

"Good plan," Kimberly said agreeably.

Mandy let out a little sigh of relief that only I caught. That's when I realized how worried she had been about keeping her friendship with Kimberly.

Just then, Lois Waller came up. Smiling, she held out her hand to me to shake. "Thanks for seconding my nomination. May the best student win. Good luck."

I thought it was really nice and sportsmanlike of her, and I returned her handshake and wished her luck, too.

Then she held out her hand to Kimberly. Kimberly looked down at the hand for a minute with this incredibly snotty look on her face. The look said, *You don't actually expect me to touch that hand, do you?*

When Kimberly made no move to shake, Mandy's cheeks turned red and she reached out and shook Lois's hand. "Good luck," she said warmly. "I think we're lucky to have four good candidates, and I'm glad you're running."

It eased the tension, and Lois smiled. "See you guys later." Then she walked off.

"Maybe Lois can run on the Save the Whales platform," Kimberly quipped.

A laugh escaped Mandy. She tried to stop it, but it came out of her nose, and she made this amused snorting sound.

I think Lois heard it, because I saw her turn around and look at us. I started banging Mandy on the back, pretending that she was choking instead of laughing.

"That was really out of line," I said angrily to Kimberly as soon as Lois had turned back down the hall.

"Oh, don't be so preachy," Kimberly said in a bored tone. "You used to laugh at Lois Waller all the time, too."

I felt a flush rising up the back of my neck. She was right. I did laugh at Lois Waller. But I was ashamed of myself now. And I thought Mandy ought to be ashamed of herself, too.

Mandy caught my reproachful look. "I've got to get to class," she said quickly. "See you guys later."

That left me and Kimberly staring each other down in front of the lockers.

There's an expression: "If you don't succeed, try, try again." I had tried to keep things with Kimberly friendly. Maybe it was time for another try. "Kimberly," I said in my nicest voice, "I really don't want to get into a big competition with you. Can't we work something out? Maybe we could be running mates or something."

Kimberly gave me a nasty smile. "Are you afraid to compete with me?"

"I'm not afraid," I said evenly. "I just don't like to see so many people get hurt. The Unicorns just got over a big fight, and now we're squaring off against each other again. The club doesn't need this."

"This *Club*," Kimberly said with a sneer, "has turned into the biggest bunch of goody-goody geek-oids I've ever seen. I think what you need is a little shaking up. A little competition. A little excitement."

A little trouble was what she meant. I sighed heavily. What is it with people like that? Why are they only happy when they've got everybody upset and angry?

I saw Rick Hunter and Denny Jacobson come out of the boys' bathroom at the end of the hall and turn in our direction.

Immediately, Kimberly leaned forward, dangled her head upside down, and then flipped her head back so that her hair stood out all full and fluffy around her face. "Hi, Rick. Hi, Denny."

The boys stopped, and it was clear from their faces that they thought Kimberly looked really great.

"I'm really happy you're back," Rick said.

"That makes two of us," Denny said.

"Thanks," Kimberly purred. "And since you feel

that way, maybe I can talk you guys into voting for me for student council."

"Count on us," Rick promised.

Denny nodded. "In fact, count on the whole soccer team. I think I can pretty much guarantee that they'll vote as a bloc."

I couldn't believe it. These were the guys who had nominated Randy Mason. Now here they were promising to vote for Kimberly. And nobody had even talked about issues yet. Or what they stood for. Or what they were prepared to do. Rick and Denny were promising to betray Randy and vote for Kimberly because she was flirty and popular.

It made me realize I was going to have to work hard to beat her. Really hard.

# Six

That same night, the Mary Wallace for Student Council campaign team met in Elizabeth Wakefield's room. On the team were me, Maria, Elizabeth, and Evie.

Jessica, Ellen, Kimberly, and Lila were on the Kimberly Haver for Student Council committee, and they were meeting downstairs in the Wakefields' living room.

Every few minutes, we'd hear a burst of laughter or high-pitched giggling from downstairs. It sounded more like a slumber party than a strategy meeting.

"Doesn't sound like they're taking this election too seriously," Evie commented wryly.

"They're not," said Elizabeth grimly. "Which is why we're going to win—if we can just come up with a platform."

Elizabeth was sitting at her desk with a pad and pencil. Evie was sitting cross-legged on the floor with another pad and pencil. Maria was sprawled across Elizabeth's bed, lying on her stomach with her pad and pencil.

And me?

I was pacing back and forth across Elizabeth's blue-carpeted room, trying to think.

Elizabeth bit her pencil and tugged on her ponytail in frustration. "Issues!" Elizabeth groaned. "We've got to come up with some issues."

"Something that kids really care about," Maria said. "Like the off-campus lunch privilege."

We all looked at each other. Then I sighed. "I've already given that some thought, and I just can't think of anything that would make Mr. Clark change his mind."

"Just because some dumb kid doesn't watch where he's going, you guys get penalized. It's not fair," Evie said.

Maria grinned. "I hate to tell you this, but . . ."

"*Life's not fair!*" we all shouted at once. Then we began to laugh.

Elizabeth tapped her pencil on her pad. "OK. Forget the off-campus lunch privilege. We need issues that are realistically negotiable. But what? How are we going to make Mary stand out?"

Elizabeth wrote "campaign issues" on her pad, then looked up thoughtfully. "Randy Mason will probably campaign on the science lab issue," she said. "Lots of the lab equipment is out of date and needs replacing."

Evie nodded. "Yeah. But most kids hate science class, so they're not going to get all fired up over getting some new beakers and a bunsen burner."

We all laughed.

"What about library books," Elizabeth suggested. "Right now there's a four-book limit on the number of books you can check out. If you're working on a heavy-duty research project, that's a pain, because you need lots of source materials."

I nodded. "That's a good one. I'll promise to try to get the limit raised."

"How about promising to try to get teachers to assign more extra credit for students who aren't doing too well?" Evie said. "Last month, when I was spending so much time getting ready for my violin recital, the only thing that got me through English was the fact that Mr. Bowman let me do some extra credit after the recital to bring up my grade."

"Bravo!" Maria, Elizabeth, and I all yelled. We stood up and gave her a standing ovation.

Evie laughed and looked pleased.

(I forgot to tell you—Evie is a brilliant violinist. When she gets out of high school, she's going to go to a music conservatory to study with some of the best violinists in the world.)

Elizabeth rapidly scribbled on her pad. "OK. This is good. We've got two really good campaign issues. But what issues do you think Lois Waller is going to run on?"

"Better food in the cafeteria?" Evie said, raising one eyebrow humorously.

In spite of ourselves, Maria, Elizabeth, and I laughed. Then Elizabeth banged her forehead down on her desk in comic punishment. "Stop it!" she said, half to herself and half to us. "We sound just like Kimberly."

There was another burst of giggles from downstairs. Then somebody put a Johnny Buck tape into the player and turned the volume up really loud.

Every smile in the room disappeared, and there was a long thoughtful silence as we listened to the music drift up toward us from the living room.

Obviously, Kimberly wasn't taking this election seriously at all. None of them were. They were just going to breeze through it on their reputations for being the in crowd.

It was sort of insulting that they seemed so sure of themselves. And a little demoralizing, too.

"Look," I said, putting my hands on my hips. "We may all be Unicorns, but for now they're the other team. And we've got to beat them. Because the only way we're ever going to keep this club together is for me to win.

"Like Elizabeth said this morning, if Kimberly wins the election, it'll give her even more influence over Jessica, Lila, and Ellen. And if that happens, I think the Unicorns are finished—at least as far as we're concerned."

Everybody's face was serious, and I could see that

they knew what I was talking about. This wasn't just a fight for the presidency of the student council anymore. It was a fight for the soul of the Unicorn Club.

The next day was Wednesday. I was late for school, because I had a dentist's appointment. By the time I got there, third period was just about over.

My dentist was in the downtown office district, and in order to get to school, I had to cross the street near the construction project. There were big trucks and workmen everywhere. Cars were speeding along this narrow little lane that detoured between the torn-up places on the street.

I had to wait and wait and wait and wait while the cars streamed by in the detour lane.

Finally, I thought it was clear. I started running across the boulevard when suddenly, from out of nowhere, this little blue car was racing toward me.

*Honk! Honk!*

Somebody grabbed my arm and yanked me out of the way so hard they nearly pulled my arm out of its socket.

"Look out, you idiot!" yelled the driver.

The hand on my arm let go, and I looked up and saw that one of the, workmen had pulled me back onto the curb. "You OK?" he asked in a shaky voice. I could tell by his face that he was scared. It had been a closer call than I realized.

"Sorry to pull you like that, but I thought that car was going to flatten you."

I rubbed my shoulder and tried to smile. "I'd rather have a sore arm than be flat as a pancake. Thanks for pulling me out of the way. I thought I was being careful, but I never saw him coming."

The man nodded in the direction of the cement mixer and gravel truck. "There are always a lot of blind spots on a construction job like this. Be careful, OK?"

I promised I would and then continued across the boulevard. But it was hard to walk. My legs were wobbling and my hands were shaking. I'd come very close to getting run over. Now I knew why Mr. Clark had forbidden us to leave campus during lunch.

It really was dangerous.

By lunchtime, it looked as though things were improving between the Unicorns. The whole club was standing near the lockers, and they all seemed to be talking at once.

But when I went over to join them, I realized it wasn't a discussion, it was an argument.

"Don't be such a wimp," Kimberly Haver was telling Maria.

"I'm not being a wimp," Maria insisted. "I'm just not going to risk getting into trouble over a slice of pizza."

"What are you guys talking about?" I asked.

"Kimberly wants to go off campus for lunch," Elizabeth answered. "She wants to go to Guido's Pizza."

"But Mr. Clark said—"

"'But Mr. Clark said,'" Kimberly interrupted

immediately, mocking my voice with a high-pitched prissy-sounding imitation.

Jessica and Ellen laughed, and I felt my face turning red. Kimberly could be so caustic sometimes. Funny. But caustic. Always at somebody else's expense.

"Listen," Kimberly said in her normal voice. "It's a stupid rule. And I don't think we should let some stupid rule stop us from going out to lunch."

I was dying to tell them that I'd nearly been hit by a car this morning. But I was afraid to say anything. I didn't want to be the target of Kimberly's sarcasm again. I guess that makes me a moral coward. But I just wasn't up to a confrontation.

Kimberly shrugged her shoulders and pushed her long hair off of her shoulder. "I'm going for pizza. Who's going with me?"

"I'm in," Jessica said immediately.

"Me too," chorused Ellen and Lila at the same time.

"Count me out," Maria said.

Elizabeth, Evie, and I didn't even bother to say anything. It was obvious what our opinion was.

Kimberly and her crew took off down the hall, looked both ways to make sure there were no teachers around, then pushed open the back doors and disappeared.

"Come on," I said quietly. "Let's go to the cafeteria."

# Seven

"Did you hear?" Caroline Pearce asked me in a breathless voice just before fifth period.

"Hear what?" I asked.

Caroline Pearce is the biggest gossip at Sweet Valley Middle School. I don't usually like to listen to gossip, but sometimes Caroline was better than a newspaper. I'm not really sure how she managed to find out all the things she knew, but she was a student messenger, and that meant she was in and out of Mr. Clark's office a lot—picking up memos for teachers and stuff. I guess she overhears a lot of conversations.

"Kimberly Haver, Lila Fowler, Jessica Wakefield, and Ellen Riteman all got caught going off campus for lunch," she said. "They're in Mr. Clark's office right now."

My stomach lurched. I felt really bad for them, and somehow, the excited glow on Caroline's face made me furious.

"Well, you don't have to sound so happy about it," I said angrily.

Caroline stepped back as if she'd been slapped. "I'm sorry. I thought you'd want to know, seeing as how you're all members of the same club."

And with that, she turned on her heel and marched off to spread the word to the rest of the school.

Just then, Elizabeth came hurrying toward me with an armload of flyers. "Here's some of your campaign materials," she said. "You take some, I'll take some, and Maria and Evie can take some. We'll pass them out between classes."

"I guess you heard about Kimberly and the others getting caught going off campus."

Elizabeth nodded. "Yep! And as much as I'm sorry to see them get into trouble, it's a good thing for us."

"It is?"

"Sure! Who would vote for Kimberly now?" Elizabeth asked. "I mean, would you vote for somebody who's just been sentenced to four hours of detention next Saturday?"

I hadn't thought about how it would affect the election. And even though it was really selfish, I couldn't help seeing Elizabeth's point and feeling good about it.

The happy glow didn't last long, though.

As it turned out, the rest of the students didn't see things the way we did.

"I say we should all form a protest," Denny Jacobson said. "Free the Sweet Valley Four," or something like that.

School was over, but lots of students were hanging around the halls talking about the big scandal of the day.

"It's a dumb rule," Aaron Dallas said. "It treats us like morons. If you ask me, I say good for Kimberly for breaking it."

"I don't know about you, but I'm voting for Kimberly in the election. At least we know she's got the guts to stand up to the administration," piped in Helen Bradley.

That did it. I had to say something. If I didn't and then someone got hurt, I'd feel guilty because I hadn't spoken up.

"The rule she broke is to protect us," I said. "This morning I was almost hit crossing the boulevard. Mr. Clark is right, it's not safe."

About fifteen pairs of hostile eyes stared at me for a long moment.

"Maybe you need to watch where you're going," Helen Bradley suggested in a sarcastic voice.

"I did. But it's really hard to see the traffic coming around the corner."

The fifteen pairs of eyes rolled upward as if to say "What a nerd!"

"Chill out, Mary," Aaron said. "You're starting to sound more like a member of the faculty than a student."

Maria pinched my arm. "Let's move out," she whispered in my ear. "I think we're losing votes here, not gaining them."

"Why are they being so childish?" I asked Maria angrily as we left the school. "It really isn't safe."

"People think it's cool to be a rebel—even when the rebel is a moron," Maria said in disgusted voice. "Now Kimberly's got that rep and so do Jessica and the others. In the meantime, we're getting a rep for being boring goody-goodies."

"So what do we do?" I asked miserably. "Go break some rule just for the sake of breaking it?"

"No," Maria answered. "I think we just have to be true to ourselves and our own code of Unicorn ethics."

"But will we win?"

"It's not whether you win or lose," Maria said. "It's how you play the game."

I stopped and glared at Maria. "That is the stupidest expression in the whole world."

"I know. But it's all I could think of on such short notice," she said glumly. "Come on. Let's go to the Center. It's Ellen, Lila, and Mandy's day to work. But they can always use an extra pair of hands. And we always seem to feel better after helping out there. Maybe we can even mend some fences."

"Fine by me," I answered.

"Let's duck into Primo's for a soda first," Maria suggested. Primo's was in the shopping area behind the school.

Maria saw the worry on my face. I didn't want to get run over. "Don't worry. If there's two of us keeping an eye out, we shouldn't have too much trouble crossing."

Primo's sounded good to me. Not only was I thirsty, I was hungry, too. The events of the morning had killed my appetite for lunch. And now my stomach was growling.

We stood impatiently on the curb, waiting for traffic to stop. Finally, one of the construction workers stopped the traffic so that we and a bunch of other kids could cross.

The noise level was incredibly high. Jackhammers. Cement mixers. Truck engines. Impatient car horns.

Primo's was only one block away, so we were there in a matter of minutes. As soon as we sat down, a waitress hurried over. A few other kids drifted in, but most kids passed on by.

"What'll it be?" she asked cheerfully.

Maria ordered a soda, and then decided to have some fries with it.

I ordered a cheeseburger and a milkshake.

The waitress wrote the order on her pad. "Little late for lunch, isn't it?" she teased. "Not that I'm complaining," she added, just in case we didn't get that she was teasing. "We're always glad to have the business. And we don't see too many kids in here at lunch anymore."

"It's because of the new rule," Maria said.

"I heard," the waitress said with a long face. "All the merchants around here have heard. And we're just as unhappy as you kids are. It's really cutting into our business."

"We'll try to make it up to you," said Maria, laughing. "I'll change that soda to a milk shake."

The waitress nodded. "Coming right up," she said, then she hurried away.

Through the plate-glass window, we saw Kimberly, Jessica, Lila, and Ellen walk by, laughing and talking.

"Guess they're on their way to the Center," Maria commented.

I didn't say anything. It felt a little forlorn sitting in Primo's with just Maria. Usually, we would have all been in there together. Sitting at the big table, laughing and joking.

"Something wrong?" Maria asked.

I forced myself to smile. I didn't tell her what I'd been thinking, because I didn't want Maria to think that her company wasn't enough for me. "No," I answered quickly. "I'm just hungry. As soon as I get something to eat, I'll be my usual perky self."

Her face still reflected concern.

I forced myself to smile brighter. "I promise."

# Eight

I guess it was around four thirty by the time we got to the Center. After wolfing down our food at Primo's, we'd stopped at the stationery store because Maria needed some school supplies. Then I ran into a friend of my mom's, and we talked for a few minutes.

Anyway, it just took us a while to get there. So we expected Lila, Ellen, and Mandy to be there when we arrived.

Guess again.

Mandy was there. But there was no sign of Ellen or Lila. And the place was in chaos.

Half the kids were crying. There were spilt milk and smushed crackers all over the floor. Allison and Sandy were whomping each other with puzzle books. And Arthur was just sitting in the playhouse screaming at the top of his lungs.

"What's going on?" I yelled to Mandy. "Where are Lila and Ellen?"

"I don't know," Mandy snapped. "And right now, I don't care. Would you please just see what you can do to get some of these kids calmed down?"

Maria immediately went to arbitrate between Sandy and Allison.

I opened the door to the playhouse and made faces at Arthur Foo until he stopped screaming and began to laugh.

Mandy got a bunch of the other kids organized around a game of Go Fish at the little round wooden table in the corner.

After about twenty minutes, things had calmed down enough that we could clean up the milk and crackers and have a little private conversation.

"Did Lila and Ellen just not show up?" I asked in disbelief.

Mandy turned an angry face toward me. "I guess they couldn't get here. I know they got into some trouble today, so maybe they're in Mr. Clark's office or something."

"No, they're not," Maria said. "I saw them leaving school around the same time we did."

"Then I guess they had something else to do," Mandy replied in a flat tone.

"Then why didn't they get word to some of the rest of us to cover for them?" Maria demanded. "Nobody can handle this bunch by themselves."

Mandy sighed. "I know. I know," she reluctantly agreed. "They should have let somebody know they weren't coming. But I guess they just forgot. It was a strange day."

There was an insistent tug on my sleeve.

I looked down and saw little Oliver Washington looking up at me with forlorn eyes. "When is Jessica coming?" he asked. "She hasn't been here since last month."

It was an exaggeration. I knew it hadn't been a month since Jessica had been here. It hadn't even been a week. But the point was, Oliver missed her.

"Jessica couldn't come today," I said. "But she'll be here again soon."

"Why couldn't she come?" he asked.

What could I say? That she was too busy fawning over Kimberly to keep her commitment to the Center? Her commitment to Oliver?

Nope. I believe in being honest with kids, but there's such a thing as being *too* honest. Maybe there was a way to explain things without hurting his feelings too much.

"We're having an election at school," I said gently. "It's really important and it's taking up a lot of time. But when it's over, we'll all be back," I promised.

"Good save," Maria murmured.

It was a good save. Everything I'd said was the truth, so my conscience was clear. I hadn't lied to a child, but I hadn't made anybody look bad, either.

Maybe I really did have a future in politics.

Oliver still looked forlorn, though. "I miss her," he said sadly. "I miss the other ones, too."

As he wandered off, Maria turned a furious face toward Mandy. "Are you telling me none of the other Unicorns besides us have been here since last week? Nobody came on Monday or Tuesday?"

"Elizabeth and Evie have been here," she said.

"But not Jessica? Or Ellen? Or Lila?"

Mandy paused for a moment, then nodded.

"That's terrible," Maria exploded. "They have a commitment here. And I don't care what else—"

Mandy held up her hands. "Can it," she said angrily. "We're going through a weird time. I'm not going to take sides. So don't try to push my buttons, OK?"

And with that, she stalked off toward the kitchenette, banged a saucepan on the counter, and began making hot chocolate.

"I can't believe Mandy," Maria whispered through gritted teeth.

"I can," I said. And I really could. Mandy was in an awful position. We were forcing her to choose between new friends and old friends. And she didn't want to do it.

I didn't blame her. I didn't want to choose, either. And if there had been any way to avoid it, I wouldn't have gotten into this situation.

But I was in it. And only a coward would back out now.

\*        \*        \*

On Thursday, my campaign team and I got to school early so we could hand out flyers at the doors.

Maria and I manned the front doors. Elizabeth and Evie manned the side doors.

"Rick!" I called out as Rick Hunter came up the front steps of the school. "I'm campaigning for student council president. Here's a flyer."

He smiled. "Thanks. But I think I've already decided who I'm going to vote for."

I sighed. He wasn't the first person who had said that to me this morning. But still, I launched into my little spiel about arranging extra-credit work for kids who needed it and raising the limit on the number of library books that could be checked out.

Rick listened politely, but I could tell that raising the limit on library checkouts wasn't thrilling him to death.

". . . so if you have a big research project . . ." I was saying.

"Hey, Kimberly," Rick yelled.

Kimberly and Jessica were coming up the walk toward the steps.

Rick just turned his back to me. Right when I was in the middle of a sentence. It was so incredibly rude, it made me want to grab the back of his shirt, shake him, and yell, "Hey, you, I was talking."

But I couldn't do that. It wouldn't win me any friends—or any votes.

Everybody in Kimberly's group was wearing T-shirts that said VOTE FOR KIMBERLY. The shirts looked fabulous, and they made me wish we had thought of something like that.

Within seconds, a crowd had gathered around Kimberly. There was a lot of cheering and hooting and laughter. I saw Maria standing in the crowd, and with a little crook of her finger, she motioned to me to come over and join the group.

I went over and stood at the perimeter of the little circle.

"That's brilliant," I heard Aaron Dallas say.

"What's he talking about?" I asked Maria.

"Kimberly says she's come up with a foolproof plan for sneaking off campus without getting caught."

I rolled my eyes. What a bunch of idiots. Were they really going to try the same stunt two days in a row?

"Kimberly says if they go through the hole in the fence on the west side of the grounds and then work their way around the hedge, they can get across the construction without being seen from any of the school windows," Maria said.

"What's up?" asked a voice in my ear.

I turned and saw Mandy looking at me with curious eyes.

"Kimberly's come up with another plan for sneaking off campus for lunch," I answered.

"Oh," Mandy said. Her eyes and voice were

completely neutral. No opinion. No response.

Before I could say anything, Mandy backed away, hurried toward the heavy double doors at the school entrance, and disappeared inside the building.

Elizabeth and Evie were coming up the front walk, and Maria and I left the crowd that had gathered around Kimberly so we could talk to them.

"What's going on?" both of them wanted to know.

We told them.

Elizabeth sighed heavily. "I hate to say this, but—"

"Kimberly just went up six points on the coolness meter," Maria finished for her.

# Nine

At lunch, there were far fewer students than normal in the cafeteria and the outside lunch area.

"She must have taken half the school with her," Evie commented as we sat down at the temporary Unicorner—a picnic table set up on the grounds behind the cafeteria.

"It's stupid," Maria said through a mouthful of sandwich. "Don't they think the teachers are going to notice that a bunch of people aren't here?"

"I don't think they think too much about the consequences of anything." Elizabeth sighed.

"I can't believe it," a voice said behind me.

I turned and saw Caroline Pearce. "How come you guys didn't go with the other Unicorns?"

Talk about pouring salt in a wound. If everybody else at the Unicorner was feeling the way I was feeling, then we were all feeling left out, boring, and abandoned.

It made me feel like kicking Caroline.

(Then that worried me. Was I developing some kind of killer instinct? Some kind of political-shark mentality? This morning I'd wanted to grab Rick Hunter and shake him. Now I had to resist the impulse to kick Caroline.)

"Mind your own business, Caroline," Elizabeth snapped.

Maria's jaw dropped and her eyes popped open wide. Evie looked as if a camera flash had just gone off right in her face. And I was so surprised, I just gaped at Elizabeth.

Being rude, or even brusque, is so far out of character for Elizabeth, I couldn't believe she had really said it.

Caroline looked incredibly offended and I squinted at Elizabeth very closely—just to make sure that it wasn't really Jessica pulling some kind of trick by imitating Elizabeth.

But it was Elizabeth, all right. And she looked mad.

"They didn't go because they're chicken," said a nasty voice at the table behind us. Then I heard the sound of a lot of boys laughing.

We all exchanged looks, but we didn't say anything.

"Cluck cluck cluck!" went Dennis Cookman.

"Let's get out of here," Elizabeth said.

As one, we all stood, took our trays over to the

disposal station, and dumped our food. None of us were hungry anymore.

"This is terrible," Elizabeth said mournfully as we left the cafeteria and walked down the main hallway to the library wing.

"We're getting reputations for being total geeks," Maria said, pounding her fist against her thigh in frustration. "And so far, Mary is the only candidate who's even tried to talk about issues. Randy hasn't passed out any platform flyers, and neither have Lois Waller or Kimberly."

"That reminds me," Elizabeth said. "We'd better get started on your speech soon."

I nodded. I wasn't too worried about standing up and giving a speech. Not with Elizabeth and Maria helping me. I was worried that the really important issues wouldn't be of any interest to anybody. That the kids would just vote for the person they thought was cool enough to stand up to Mr. Clark and go off campus anyway. And obviously, that person was Kimberly.

We had just turned the corner when we stopped dead in our tracks and gasped in surprise.

Coming down the hall was Mr. Clark. And behind him, there was a long line of students. Kimberly Haver was at the head of the line. Then Jessica. Lila. Ellen. And about fifteen other kids.

Obviously, they'd been caught.

Mr. Clark opened the door of his office and then made a sweeping gesture with his hand. "Everybody inside. And I advise you to cancel any weekend plans you have for the next month. Because you're all going to have Saturday detentions. Lots of them."

*Finally*, I thought, *Kimberly has gone too far*. Not only had she gotten herself into trouble. She had gotten a bunch of other kids in trouble, too.

Surely her popularity would fall now.

When the last bell rang, signaling that school was over, the hallways echoed with indignant voices and hushed conversations.

Elizabeth and Maria fell into step beside me as I walked down the hall toward the exit.

"We should have known she'd get us in trouble . . ." one girl was saying behind me.

". . . why I ever let myself get talked into . . ." came floating over the hum of voices.

". . . those Unicorns. Trust them to mess everything up," somebody else grumbled.

"I hate to gloat," Maria said with a smile as we made our way through the thick crowd of students. "But I think Kimberly Haver just blew her campaign out of the water."

"Sounds that way to me," Elizabeth agreed. "Everybody likes a rebel—until that rebel gets them sentenced to a string of Saturday detentions. I'll bet they don't think Kimberly is so glamorous anymore. I'll bet they think she's a jerk."

I hated it that so many kids had gotten into trouble. But it was the best thing that could have happened to me as far as the campaign for student council went.

Maria and Elizabeth pushed open the heavy double doors at the front of the school, and we stepped out onto the front steps.

Kimberly, Jessica, Lila, and Ellen were all gathered there with a lot of other kids. Some of them were kids who had gotten into trouble that afternoon.

The minute I appeared, Kimberly's eyes met mine and her face flushed with rage.

"That's the rat," she said, pointing an accusing finger in my direction. "That's the goody-goody squealer that told Mr. Clark what we were doing."

Every eye was on me. And every eye looked furious.

I was so stunned, I just froze. I couldn't believe it. I was in total shock. It was so bizarre and unexpected and horrible, I couldn't even find the voice to deny it.

"See?" Kimberly said, taking advantage of my dumbfounded silence. "She's not even bothering to deny it."

"That's a lie," Maria said angrily.

"Mary would never do something like that," Elizabeth retorted. "Would you, Mary?"

My Adam's apple felt so big, it was almost choking me. Hot tears stung my eyes and my lower lip was quivering. *Please don't let me cry in front of all these people,* I pleaded mentally. *Please don't let me cry.*

"She's probably the one that told before, too," a voice in the crowd said.

"Goody-goodies," another disgusted voice commented.

"She did it because she thought Mr. Clark would disqualify me as a student council candidate," Kimberly said in a theatrical voice that practically vibrated with righteous indignation. It was as if she thought she was Patrick Henry or something.

"But her plan failed," Kimberly continued. "Mr. Clark has not disqualified me. So read my lips, Mary Wallace: this is war!"

That did it. My Adam's apple was back to its normal size, and I didn't feel like crying anymore. I felt like screaming. I felt like punching. But I decided to settle for shouting. "If you want a war, Kimberly Haver," I shouted, "you've got one."

"We'll grind you goody-goodies into the dust," Jessica yelled.

"Speaking of dust, don't forget to eat ours," Elizabeth bellowed at her sister.

There was a lot of appreciative laughter and some scattered applause. I wasn't sure who it was for, but I hoped it was for Elizabeth and her quick reply.

I was just getting wound up to deliver a few insults of my own when I saw Mandy. She had been standing off to the side, not taking part at all.

Her face looked stricken. And the next thing I knew, she was hurrying away. She practically ran down the front steps of the school and started down the long walkway that led to the street.

I didn't know what to do. Go comfort Mandy? Stay and insult Kimberly some more? Or just leave?

More people had come out of the building now, and there seemed to be two camps forming. Those who thought Kimberly was a big hero for what she had tried to do. And those who thought she was childish and irresponsible.

Maria, Elizabeth, and Evie had picked up the fight, and somehow, nobody seemed to be paying any attention to me anymore.

So I left. I just walked away from the squabbling, angry, shouting group of students.

This thing was getting way out of hand. It was a million times worse than when we'd fought over boyfriends. Then it was just boys that came between us. But this time the problem is us—who we are, what we think is important. Could everyone forgive and forget when the election was all over?

Or would the Unicorns split up again, this time for good?

# Ten

Getting across the boulevard was hard by myself. But I managed to make it without waiting too long, and then I headed for Primo's. It looked pretty empty, so I walked in and found a booth way in the back. I could still see out the front window, but I didn't feel like talking to anybody. Not even my good friends. I couldn't get over worrying about Mandy. Most of all, I couldn't believe the way we were all behaving.

Elizabeth had suddenly started being rude. Maria was gloating over other people's misfortunes.

And Evie?

Well, Evie seemed pretty much unchanged. But she was younger than we were. And impressionable. I couldn't help feeling that we were setting a poor example.

No, I decided. I wasn't going to make Kimberly Haver eat my dust. I was going to conduct my campaign like a lady. Like a professional. Like a grown-up.

I wasn't going to trade insults with the opposition. And I wasn't going to respond to any more ridiculous accusations.

"Hello? Anybody home?"

A hand passed down over my eyes.

I looked up and saw the waitress smiling at me. "I thought maybe you were in a trance," she explained. "You've been staring at that same spot on the wall ever since you sat down."

"I was just thinking," I said.

"While you're at it, see if you can think us up some business."

"Is it that bad?" I asked.

The waitress nodded. "Not only is that road construction ruining *us*, it's ruining the ice cream parlor. And the comic book stand. And the pizza place. Basically, every merchant in this area that depends on pedestrian traffic from the boulevard is hurting. We had hoped that we could make up the business with the lunchtime crowd from the school. But now that's out of the question."

"I never realized how important we were to the businesspeople around here," I said.

"Believe me. You're important. But safety comes first. Your principal called all the store owners around here and asked us to refuse service to any student who was here at lunchtime. So don't come sneaking in here at lunch, because you'll just go back to school hungry."

Before I could respond, the little bell on the door tinkled, and a crossing guard came in and sat at the counter.

"How are you, Ray?" the waitress said, hurrying to get him a cup of coffee.

"Just fine," Ray answered.

"Something to eat?"

Ray shook his head. "Don't have time. I'm due at the North Loop intersection in fifteen minutes. There's a lot of traffic there, and they need somebody to direct the traffic and help the pedestrians get across."

Suddenly, I began to get the glimmer of an idea. I gulped down my soda, paid, and left a good tip. Then I walked out and looked at the car Ray had parked beside the curb. "Perkins Security," it said across the side.

Obviously, Ray worked for a private security firm.

"Sure. We could probably survive the construction if we could get more lunch business," said the manager of the ice cream parlor. "And the lunch crowd is important. We don't get many kids in here after school, because most students enter and exit from the front of the school. And all the residential sections are in the other direction."

The man took a rag and began to wipe the already spotless counter. "But your principal doesn't want you kids crossing that boulevard at lunchtime. And as much as I want to sell ice cream, it's not worth somebody getting hurt."

"So what will you do?" I asked.

The manager let out a long sigh. "I don't know. I really don't know." He swept his arm around the room. It was mostly empty. "All I know is that if this is the best I can do, I won't last another two months. I won't even make enough to pay the light bill, never mind rent, salaries, supplies, and all the rest of it."

I bought an ice cream cone—just to make him feel better. Then I said good-bye and headed for the comic book stand.

"I'd say business is off forty percent," the manager of the comic stand said. He had a stack of new comics in his arms, and he was trying to jam them into the already stuffed racks.

"Usually, I can't keep these racks full. Now, I don't have room for the new comics when they come in."

"Why is business so bad?" I asked, even though I knew the answer.

The man gestured toward the boulevard. "That construction cuts off all the pedestrian traffic coming from two directions."

"What if the kids were allowed to leave school during lunchtime again? Could you sell enough comics to stay in business until the construction is finished?"

The man chewed the inside of his cheek for a moment as he thought about it. The he gave a little brisk nod of his head. "I could," he said firmly. "But your principal has asked us not to sell to, or serve, any kids from the middle school at lunchtime."

"What if that rule changed?"

The man's face broke into a broad smile.

That night, we had a campaign strategy meeting in Elizabeth's bedroom. We sat on the floor surrounded by index cards and spiral notebooks full of notes. All around us, there were wads of balled-up paper with discarded drafts of our letters and proposals.

Just as before, we were working hard to plot our strategy. And just as before, the competition seemed to be goofing and fooling around downstairs. Now they were listening to records again.

It was strange. I mean, we were all Unicorns. Friends who had come through for one another time and time again. But now the club was split right down the middle. Possibly for good.

Both camps had declared war this afternoon. According to Elizabeth, she and Jessica weren't even speaking. But here we were, all gathered under one roof. It was only a matter of time before somebody fired the first shot.

"Mary, you're brilliant!" Maria said in a happy voice after I had outlined my plan. After I'd seen the crossing guard that afternoon, I'd hit on the answer. Hire someone to help students cross the street safely!

"I knew you'd be a good candidate," Evie said enthusiastically. "I just knew it."

"It's about time one of us put on her thinking cap," Elizabeth said. "I'm just embarrassed I didn't think of it myself. I got so caught up in the heat of the campaign, it short-circuited my common sense."

"This way, the kids get what they want—their off-campus lunch privilege. Plus, the school and the PTA can relax, and we'll be doing something good for our local economy," I said.

"But will the school agree to spend the money?" Maria asked.

"Not according to my dad. He's on the PTA, and he says the school district doesn't have an extra cent in the budget," Elizabeth answered.

"The school doesn't have to pay," I said. "The merchants will pay."

"They will?" Evie asked.

I nodded. "I think so. They're all complaining that business is off because of the construction. They were counting on business from the school to get them through the next several months."

"Great! So what's the next step?" Maria asked.

"The next step is to call Perkins Security and find out how much it would cost to hire a crossing guard for a couple of hours in the afternoon. Then we need to canvass the local merchants and see how many would be willing to pitch in to hire him. I think that probably all of them will want to. In the long run, it will help them, because they'll get a lot of business from the students."

"A crossing guard ought to satisfy everybody's safety concerns, too," Elizabeth said.

I nodded. "I'll call tomorrow morning and get the information on the guard. And tomorrow afternoon, let's all split up to interview the merchants."

Somebody downstairs turned up the volume on the stereo so that the bass thumped all through the house and we could hardly hear each other speak.

There it was. The first shot.

In retaliation, Elizabeth angrily got up and jumped up and down—hard—on the floor of her room, which was the ceiling of the living room.

The volume was turned down. But a loud burst of laughter let us know that somebody had said something mean about us.

"Ughhh," Maria said. "They make me so mad."

I held up my hands. "Me, too. But it's best if we try not to be angry at the others," I said. "We'll all do a better job of campaigning if we try to stay friends. After all, we're a club. And I hope we'll be a club again after all this is over. Even if it takes a little bending on our part—OK, a lot of bending—I say we should still try to be friends."

There was a long pause while everybody thought it over.

Elizabeth said nothing, but she took a deep

breath and looked at the ceiling, which meant that she was thinking about it.

But Maria folded her arms across her chest, and Evie did the same. Body-language-wise, they were telling me to forget it.

"Please," I begged.

Maria and Evie looked at each other. But neither relented.

"I'm not sure we're a club anymore," Maria said.

"And if we are a club, I'm not sure I want to belong to it," Evie added.

I had a sudden picture of Mandy's face. The way she'd looked this afternoon when the fight had gotten so out of control. Like her heart was breaking.

We had to stay together as a club. We just had to. Not just for Mandy's sake, but for all of our sakes.

Sure, maybe Mandy felt a little more torn than the rest of us, but we all needed to care. *United we stand, divided we fall*, I thought.

"Families fight," I said quietly. "But that doesn't mean they don't care about one another. You guys know how my mom left me with a friend when I was really little. And how I was in foster care for years. Now we're together, but we're two very different people. And we have fights—sometimes big ones. But we're still family. I still love her. And she still loves me."

Evie's eyes dropped to her lap as she listened.

"So let's not think of the Unicorns as a broken-up club. Let's think of ourselves as being in the middle of a family fight. We may shout and yell, but we're still a family. I mean, a club."

Maria's shoulders and face had relaxed a little and her brow wasn't wrinkled in a frown.

Elizabeth was nodding, so I knew she agreed with me.

Evie leaned over and put her arm around my shoulders. "You're right. You're absolutely right. I've been so miserable, thinking that this club was coming apart. I don't know what I would have done without it. The Unicorn Club made me feel like I fit in at school right away. It made me feel less like the new kid. Less like an outsider."

"So are we all OK on this?" I asked.

"OK," everybody echoed. Then we had a group high five.

"So," Elizabeth said, "where were we?"

"We were figuring out who was going to do what tomorrow," Maria answered.

I sat down and settled myself more comfortably. "I'm going to call the security company and find out how much the guard costs. You guys are going to interview the merchants and see whether or not they'll agree to cover the cost."

"Hold it," Elizabeth said suddenly.

"What?"

"Tomorrow's my day to volunteer at the Center. Maria's, too."

I sighed.

"Maybe . . ." Evie began tentatively.

We looked at her.

She bit her lip in hesitation, then she blurted out, "Maybe Jessica or Lila or Ellen would switch with you."

Everybody exchanged a look.

"It would be kind of a test," Elizabeth said.

"She's right," Maria added in a grim voice. "A test of whether or not the others can rise above our current problems and still behave like a club. A test of our true solidarity."

I ran my hand nervously through my hair. They were right. It would be a test. "Who wants to go ask them?"

There weren't any volunteers.

"OK," I sighed. "I'll go myself."

I left Elizabeth's room, walked out on the landing, and slowly descended the stairs. I stood in the living room doorway for a couple of seconds watching Kimberly, Jessica, Ellen, and Lila laughing and dancing around to the music.

Then they saw me and froze.

Jessica went over and turned off the tape. "Yes?" she said in this real nasty voice.

"I just came down to see if a couple of you guys can do us a favor."

A she's-got-to-be-kidding look spread from face to face.

"After all," I said softly, "we are all still Unicorns, aren't we?"

That got to Lila and Jessica. I could tell by their faces.

"What do you want?" Lila asked in a voice that actually sounded polite.

"I really need Elizabeth and Maria to do some research for me tomorrow, but it's their day to volunteer at the Center. I was wondering if any of you would switch days with them so they can do it."

Jessica's face lost its tight look, and so did Lila's. Lila was actually nodding. "I don't mind—" she began.

But Kimberly cut her off. "Forget it," she barked.

Lila's and Jessica's heads snapped in her direction. They both looked a little startled by Kimberly's hostile response.

"Why should we help a bunch of goody-goodies?" Kimberly sneered.

"Because we're members of the same club," I explained, trying to keep my voice pleasant.

"Members of the same club don't rat on one another."

"What do you mean by that?" I asked quietly.

There was a long, long silence.

"I mean the answer is no," Kimberly said. I looked at Jessica and Lila and Ellen, but they didn't say anything.

I sighed, turned away, and trudged back up the stairs. The split between us was worse than I had thought.

"Well?" Maria asked.

I shook my head. "They won't cooperate."

"Well, I said it before, and I'll say it again," Maria said. "They make me sooo mad."

"They're just angry because they think I got them into trouble. I guess if our positions were reversed, I'd be acting the same way. Let's just forget about it, OK? I can do the legwork myself tomorrow after school."

"I'll cancel my violin lesson tomorrow afternoon," Evie said. "Then I can help you."

"Don't do that," I answered. "Your whole future depends on those lessons. I can canvass the store owners myself. Don't sweat it."

"How are you going to talk them all into spending the money?" Elizabeth asked. "My dad says fund-raising is the hardest job in the world."

I shrugged. "I'll just do the best I can. But one of us had better call Mrs. Willard and tell her that after tomorrow, we're going to have to take a short break from our volunteer work until after the election."

# Eleven

"Mary! Mary, wait up!"

It was the next day. A Friday.

I turned around and saw Randy Mason running down the hall after me. First period had just ended, and I was on my way to my locker.

Randy came weaving and bobbing through the crowd. By the time he caught up with me, his glasses were lopsided and his pens were loose in his pocket protector. "Can I talk to you for two minutes?"

"Sure."

I thought maybe he wanted to talk about campaign issues—tell me what issues he planned to focus on so we didn't wind up running on the same platform.

"I just wanted to tell you I'm pulling out of the student council race."

"You're pulling out?" I repeated in a surprised voice.

He nodded. "The more I thought about it, the more I realized that I just don't have time. I was class president last year, and I worked with the student council a lot. People don't realize what a big job being student council president is. Everybody thinks it's just some honorary thing. But it's a lot of work, and it takes a lot of time."

I believed him. I wasn't even on the student council yet, and I was already devoting hours of time to thinking about school issues.

"Don't you like the work?" I asked. I really wanted to know, because so far, I'd regarded this whole thing as a big competition with Kimberly Haver. A fight for the hearts and minds of Jessica, Lila, and Ellen.

I hadn't given a lot of thought to the long-term demands of the job.

"I do like being part of student government," Randy said. "It's a way to feel like you're doing something good for your school. But this year, I'd rather devote that time to my lab experiments."

(Remember, I told you before, Randy is a big science fiend.)

"I'm doing two independent research projects in addition to the course work," he explained.

"You wouldn't by any chance be working on some Dr. Hyde and Mr. Jekyll formula, would you?" I joked. "Something that turns mean people into nice people?"

Randy grinned. "No. But if I could, I would. The world would never have another war."

*And the Unicorns would still be one big happy club,* I thought.

"Good luck with your experiments," I said, holding out my hand to shake his.

He took my hand and shook it. "Good luck with your campaign."

"Can I count on your vote, now that you're not running against me?"

Randy shrugged. "I don't know. Depends on what the opposition has to offer."

The bell rang, and Randy hurried off.

Even though he hadn't promised to vote for me, I knew I'd get his vote after I made my campaign speech and unveiled my plan. Because if everything worked out, by the time I made my campaign speech, I would have come up with a way to solve the biggest problem at Sweet Valley Middle School.

I had called Perkins Security that morning and found out how much it would cost to hire the crossing guard at lunchtime. The price was reasonable. And if it was divided up among a lot of different shops or restaurants, no one would have to pay much at all. The money they'd make off the students would be much more than their share of the cost.

I started walking, hurrying along the hallway on my way to second period.

I turned the corner and screeched to a stop. My jaw dropped. I couldn't believe what I saw.

There was a giggling sound, and I caught a glimpse of Lila and Ellen disappearing around the corner—so I knew who was responsible for the incredibly insulting poster that had been tacked to the bulletin board.

It was a caricature of Lois Waller. And it depicted her as a big hippopotamus waving a little flag and wearing a campaign hat.

The caption read: "Hippos belong in the zoo, not running the student council."

Somebody behind me began to laugh. I turned and saw Dennis Cookman and Alex Betner. Both of them were giggling.

"Looks just like her," Alex said.

"Looks better," Dennis quipped.

Two sixth graders whose names I didn't know came over, and one of them doubled over with laughter.

Then a small knot of sixth-grade girls appeared, to see what all the commotion was about. They took one look at the poster and began laughing and pointing.

That got the attention of a group of eighth-grade boys passing by, and when they saw the poster, they all began making snorting noises that were supposed to be hippopotamus voices. "Vote for me, snort snort," said one boy.

I felt like screaming. How could they all be so cruel? It was as if Kimberly and her group were turning the whole school into a mean and ugly mob.

"Did you draw that?" Dennis asked me with a note of real admiration in his voice.

"No, I didn't," I shouted. "And if you want to know," I added, barely able to keep from strangling someone, "I don't think it's a bit funny."

"I don't think it's a bit funny," one of the boys mimicked in a prissy falsetto.

"The rules are for your own safety," somebody else said in a silly voice.

"Vote for Mary Wallace," Dennis Cookman quipped. "It's the next-best thing to voting for your mother."

I backed up against the wall and stared in shock at the group of kids who were gathered. Every one of them was laughing and giggling—*at me*. Right to my face.

Wasn't anybody going to stand up for me? Or for Lois?

Then the bell rang, and the crowd began to break up. As the knot of people in front of me drifted off to class, I heard a choking sound. Then I saw the saddest thing I had ever seen in my whole life. I hope I never *ever* see anything like it again.

Standing there, all by herself, just behind where the crowd had been, stood Lois Waller. She'd seen it all. Heard it all.

My heart began to ache, and I forgot about my own humiliation when I saw how devastated she was.

She was in bad shape, all right. Her face was dead white. Her eyes were welling up with tears. I could see her swallowing hard, trying not to cry.

I felt so sorry for Lois, so humiliated by what had been said about me, and so angry at Lila and Ellen, I didn't know what to say.

But I did know what to do.

I reached up and tore the poster off the wall. There was a loud and very satisfying ripping sound as it came down, leaving the edges of the paper stuck to the wall with tape.

I couldn't find a trash can, so I balled it up and stuffed it down into my backsack.

"That's it," Lois said in a hoarse voice. "I can't stand any more of this. I'm dropping out. And if I were you, I'd drop out, too."

"Lois!" I cried. "We can't do that. We can't let them bully and intimidate you or me into dropping out of the race."

"You can fight back," Lois said. "You have friends. You're pretty and popular. But I'm not."

I looked at Lois. Her pudgy face. Her round figure. Her thick ankles. Yes, Lois was fat. But she was a person, and she had feelings. What Ellen and Lila had done wasn't just mean. It was cruel.

Lois turned and walked away. I wished I could think of something to say to her. Something that would help. But there was nothing I could say.

There was one thing I could do, though.

I could stay in the race . . . and win.

\*　　\*　　\*

"Here's your stuff," Elizabeth gasped, out of breath. She gave me a stack of mimeographed proposals to hand out to all the restaurant and shop owners I would be talking to.

I'd written out my proposal in the form of a letter addressed "Dear Merchant." Actually, I didn't write it all by myself. Elizabeth helped. After all, she's the best writer in the whole school.

Elizabeth had her dad read the letter over, and he said it looked very professional and well thought out. He's a lawyer, so he should know.

Elizabeth grinned at me as I tucked the letters into my backpack. Then she gave me a little wave as she hurried back down the steps. "I'm going to be late to the Center," she called out over her shoulder. "But good luck. I hope they go for it."

"You bet I'll go for it," said the manager of Primo's.

It was my first stop. The nice waitress was there, and luckily, so was the owner and manager. His name was Mr. Feldman.

He was kind of an old guy, and I was afraid he might not even listen to what I had to say. So my voice was a little nervous and shaky when I asked if I could have five minutes of his time.

He turned out to be really nice, though. He treated me like a grown-up. He even called me "Ms. Wallace" instead of "little girl."

I had given him a copy of my letter, and Mr.

Feldman glanced over it again. Then he shot a look at me. "Ms. Wallace, did you think this up?" he asked.

I nodded my head. "Yes, sir."

"You're a bright young woman." He shook his head. "Such a practical solution. We had a local Merchants' Association meeting last week. Not one person came up with this idea. Such a good solution to a difficult problem. And so simple," he repeated in a pleased voice.

"A wheel is simple, too," I joked. "But think what a big innovation it must have seemed like to the cavemen."

Mr. Feldman and the waitress both laughed appreciatively.

"So you would agree to pay the amount specified in the letter?" I asked, just to make sure.

Mr. Feldman nodded his head.

"Would you mind signing this, then?" I handed him a clipboard with a copy of the letter. Below the copy, we had drawn several lines so that people could sign the letter as if it were a contract.

Mr. Feldman took a pen from his pocket and hastily scrawled his name along the bottom. He handed me back the clipboard, then snapped his fingers as if he had just gotten a great idea. "I'm going to give you the names of a couple of other shop owners who'll probably like this idea."

He pulled a napkin out of the holder and wrote down the name of the manager of the ice cream parlor and the name of the owner of the athletic-shoe store. Then he pulled a little book from his back pocket. He looked up a few names and scribbled some more.

"I'm giving you their home numbers in case they're not in their stores. If they tell you they're busy or don't have time to talk, tell them you talked to me and I sent you over."

"Thanks," I said. "Would you mind doing me one more favor?"

"What's that?" he asked.

"Would you mind keeping this plan sort of secret for the next few days? I'm running for student council president. If I can get everybody to cooperate and get the off-campus lunch privilege back, I think it will give people a very good reason to vote for me."

Mr. Feldman put his hand on my shoulder. "Young lady, if I could come over there and vote, I'd vote for you in a second. I'll keep quiet. No problem." He gave me a broad grin. "And who knows, if all of your ideas are as good as this one, maybe I'll get to vote for you for president someday."

As I walked out of Primo's, my depression was disappearing fast. I felt happy and excited.

I was on the right track now. All I had to do was keep moving forward.

By six o'clock, I had twenty commitments. The comic book stand. The video arcade. Two shoe stores. The pharmacy. The bookstore. The card shop. And a bunch of restaurants and fast-food places.

I talked to eighteen owners or managers personally and got them all to sign the agreement (and keep quiet).

Two I was only able to reach on the phone, so I couldn't get their signatures. But they loved the idea and promised to participate.

Every single shop or restaurant owner I talked to thought my idea was brilliant. A lot of them wanted to give me money right then and there. I didn't take it, of course. The whole thing still had to be presented in my campaign speech and approved by Mr. Clark, the PTA, and the school board.

But I couldn't imagine any reason they wouldn't go for it.

There's a little park just a couple of blocks from my house and only one block from where Mandy lives. As I walked by it, I saw Mandy sitting on a park bench. She was alone, feeding the pigeons. She looked just about as sad and lonely as a person could look.

She didn't hear me coming, so she jumped in surprise when I plopped down beside her and said, "Hi!"

Mandy looked at me, gave me half a smile, said a listless "Hello," then turned her attention back to the pigeons.

"What's the matter?" I asked.

"What's the matter?" she repeated, her eyes

wide with disbelief. "How can you ask me what's the matter? The matter is that the Unicorn Club is split down the middle. I'm the president, and I have no idea how to put it back together or how to make peace."

Last night, I'd been ready to bury the hatchet if the other girls were willing. But after what had happened at school, I didn't think I could do that anymore. What they had done was just wrong. Wrong! Wrong! Wrong!

"I think you have to take a stand," I said quietly.

Mandy rubbed her forehead. "How can I when I don't know where I stand?" she demanded, exasperated. "All along I've said a good club is a club that brings out the best qualities in its members. And I don't see that happening. On Kimberly's team or yours. Look at the way you're all behaving. Even Elizabeth was shouting—and at Jessica, no less—right in front of school."

All right. She had a point. I'd even had those same thoughts myself. But there was a big difference. For Elizabeth, Maria, me, and Evie, hurling insults like that was completely out of character. Lila, Ellen, and Jessica, on the other hand, weren't exactly known for holding their tongues. Mandy knew that as well as I did.

"Mandy Miller," I said in a firm voice, "how can you say you don't know where you stand? If you know right from wrong, you know where you stand."

Mandy moved slightly away. "Please don't give

me any speeches," she muttered in a weary voice.

"All right," I said angrily. "I don't have to say anything else. A picture's worth a thousand words." I leaned over and pulled the wadded-up poster out of my backpack. I uncrumpled it and smoothed it out, but after I'd done that, it was still there. That cruel, awful cartoon of Lois Waller.

I thrust it under Mandy's face. "*That* is Kimberly Haver's idea of a campaign poster," I said, my voice shaking with anger. "I saw Lila and Ellen putting it up. Are you going to tell me you don't have an opinion about that?"

Mandy crumpled the paper up and threw it angrily toward a nearby trash can. "OK. So it's dirty politics. Real-life elections get ugly. Why should school elections be any different?"

I stared at Mandy. "I can't believe you. I can't believe you're not going to take a stand. That you're just going to shrug your shoulders and say, 'That's politics.' You're our president. You should set an example. Sure you should be impartial. Sure you should be fair. But at some point you have to do what's right."

Mandy stood. "That's what I'm trying to do!" she bellowed in an enraged voice. She leaned over and yanked a crumpled-up piece of paper out of her backpack. She uncrumpled and smoothed it with shaking hands, then held it up in front of me. "Here. It might interest you to know that I ripped this off the wall outside the library.

It was a cartoon picture of me, and I had been depicted as a rat. My hands flew to my face. Who had seen it? And were people going to believe it?

"I can't believe they'd do that to me," I said in a hushed voice.

"*They* didn't," Mandy said in a voice heavy with irony.

"Huh?"

Mandy pulled another piece of paper out of her backpack. When she uncrumpled that and held it up, I saw that it was a picture of Kimberly Haver. She had been drawn to look like the Pied Piper, leading a bunch of kids over a cliff.

I shook my head. "I don't understand. Who drew that poster?"

"The same person who drew the poster of you," Mandy said impatiently.

I stared at her, still not understanding.

"Lois Waller!" Mandy yelled, waving her arms in the air. "Lois Waller put these two posters up this morning."

"Why?" I said, confused.

"To discredit you. And to discredit Kimberly. Kimberly was just retaliating when she put up that poster of Lois."

"Are you sure it was Lois?"

"I saw her with my own eyes. So don't give me any more goody-goody lectures."

Coming from Mandy Miller, that goody-goody remark felt like a slap in the face. I snapped back, and Mandy immediately looked ashamed.

"I'm sorry," she said softly. "I didn't mean to . . ."

"Forget it."

Mandy stared at me for a long time, as though she wasn't sure whether or not she could trust me.

Finally, she decided to speak up. "Yeah, I know that what Kimberly and her friends did was mean. And I don't believe two wrongs make a right. But let's face it, Lois asked for it. She shouldn't have put up those posters in the first place."

Mandy sat back down, folded her arms angrily across her chest, and stared at the pigeons that were running around at our feet.

Somehow, I just couldn't make myself get angry with Lois. I felt sorry for her. Sorry that she felt she had to stoop so low to get some votes. Sorry that everybody always made fun of her.

"I still think you should take a stand," I said quietly.

"What?"

"I still think you should tell Kimberly, Jessica, Ellen, and Lila that what they did was nasty and mean. And that if they don't shape up, we're going to . . . suspend them or something." I paused, then went on. "It doesn't matter who started it. What matters is how we behave. We're a club, and the behavior of one group of members reflects poorly on all of us."

"Why should *I* tell them?"

"Because *you're* the president."

"I'm seriously thinking of resigning."

"That's funny, I never thought of you as a coward before," I said without missing a beat.

Mandy turned and glared at me. But I didn't pay any attention.

"How can a club or organization get through bad times if people don't stand up for what's right?"

Mandy hung her head.

"The character of a club is only as solid as the character of its members. What does that make us if even our president turns her back on difficult confrontations?"

"I don't care what you say. I'm going to stay neutral. I hate what Kimberly and her group are doing, but I don't know how to stop them, and I sure can't change them."

"I don't think you have to change them," I responded slowly. I reminded her of all the times we'd seen Lila rocking Ellie McMillan. And how Jessica had heroically rescued Peppermint, the day-care center's cat, during a thunderstorm. Or Ellen reading to a rapt audience of children—and doing all the voices of the characters, too.

Mandy looked confused.

"I guess what I'm trying to say is that Jessica, Lila, and Ellen all have good character traits. I've seen them, and so have you. But somehow Kimberly has managed to make them ashamed of those qualities. Under the right set of circumstances, I think we'll see those traits again."

"So you think things will get back to normal after the election?" she asked miserably.

"If I win, yes," I answered. I wasn't sure whether I really believed it or not. But I was determined to think positively. In spite of everything, I wanted us all to make up and be friends again. I nodded my head.

"OK," she sighed. "I guess I'm still the president of the Unicorns. But I'm sorry, Mary, I'm just not going to take a side in this. I don't think that's my job."

"Then I guess I'm sorry, too," I said, standing up. "Because I think it is your job."

Mandy gave me a long stare. But she didn't say a thing.

As I walked away, I couldn't help feeling vaguely disappointed in Mandy. Surprised, too. I had always thought I could depend on Mandy to do the right thing.

# Twelve

"You left out Victor's Video Arcade," Maria said, sitting cross-legged on Elizabeth's bed and looking over her shoulder.

"Darn!" Elizabeth exclaimed.

It was Sunday night, and Elizabeth, Maria, Evie, and I had been working all weekend on my speech.

Election day was on Thursday, but we all had tests and things over the coming week, so we were trying to get as much done tonight as possible.

I looked at the clock. It was almost eight. Evie's grandmother was going to pick us all up at eight-thirty and drive us home. Elizabeth's hands flickered over the keypad.

"Oh, double dog darn!" she shouted.

"What happened?" Maria asked.

"I accidentally deleted a paragraph."

Maria rubbed Elizabeth's shoulders like a fight trainer. "Don't worry about it. You're the champ. You know you can do it. Just pretend it's one of those hard-hitting news features you write for the school paper."

Elizabeth's face relaxed and she smiled. "That's not too tough to imagine. This is a hard-hitting speech." She tore a page off the printer. "Go over the opening part," Elizabeth urged.

I stood up straighter, trying to pretend I was in front of an audience. "I'm not going to stand up here and talk about what I plan to do," I read. "I'm going to talk about what I've already done. And what I've already done is work out a practical way for the seventh- and eighth-grade students to get their off-campus lunch privilege back."

I held up a piece of paper. "What I'm holding here is a signed agreement from the owner of Primo's Burger Shop promising to . . ."

Well, I won't bore you with the whole thing. I couldn't even if I wanted to. The whole thing wasn't finished yet. But the part that I read sounded really good.

"Bravo, bravo," Elizabeth cheered when I finished. "I don't see how you can lose."

"Are you crazy?" Evie shouted angrily at Elizabeth. She jumped up, knocked wood on the desk, and then pretended to spit between her fingers. "Don't say things like that. It's like asking for trouble."

Maria laughed, and so did I.

Elizabeth laughed, and it made her push the wrong button again. "Darn, darn, darn!" she yelled. "I took out another line I didn't mean to."

"See?" Evie said seriously.

"I thought only people in show business were superstitious," Maria said.

"I guess I get it from my grandmother, then," Evie responded. "I know most of it is silly. But believe me, with important things like this, I don't take chances."

"OK. I need some quiet now," Elizabeth said. She squinted at the monitor, her fingers moving carefully over the keypad. Maria watched over her shoulder, holding my notes and feeding her the details and numbers.

I looked over Maria's shoulder, making sure the notes and details were accurate.

The next half hour seemed like five minutes. Pretty soon Mrs. Wakefield was calling us from downstairs, telling us that Evie's grandmother was here.

We all began to gather our things. Elizabeth pulled the speech from the printer. "It needs some polishing," she said. "And you need to rehearse it."

"Rehearse it? You mean the whole thing?"

"Of course," Maria said. "You did great just now. But you were just reading it. If you do that on Thursday, you'll be totally boring. You have to practice making your voice rise and fall at the right time so that it seems like you aren't reading at all. And you need some hand gestures."

"You need to look confident up there," Elizabeth said.

"OK," I said. "When can we get together?"

"Wednesday night is the only time I can really spend on it," Elizabeth said. "I've got tests Tuesday and Wednesday, which means I'll be studying Monday and Tuesday nights."

We both shot a questioning look at Maria and Evie. Evie said she had an English test.

"Sorry." Maria shook her head regretfully. "I've got an algebra exam on Thursday, and algebra is not my best sport. That means from now until next Thursday I eat, sleep, and breathe algebra."

"But how will I rehearse without you?" I was starting to feel a little panicky.

Maria reached for her jacket. "No sweat. Elizabeth can coach you."

"I can?" Elizabeth said in a surprised voice.

"Sure. You've given speeches before."

"I know but—"

"You're the writer, Elizabeth. When you start listening to Mary deliver the speech you've written, you'll know whether or not she's emphasizing the right words. Giving enough weight to the information. Because in your head"—Maria tapped her temple—"you've been delivering this speech yourself. Haven't you?"

Elizabeth smiled. "How did you know?"

"Because whenever I got a script to look at, I couldn't resist playing other people's parts in front of the mirror at home—just for fun."

Maria reached out and slapped Elizabeth's hand. Then she slapped mine and Evie's. "Good luck."

"Evie's grandmother has been waiting for five minutes," said an impatient voice at the door.

We looked over and saw Jessica glowering at us from the doorway. "Mom sent me up to tell you guys to hurry."

Elizabeth immediately picked the speech up off the desk and held it protectively against her chest.

"Oh, don't flatter yourselves," Jessica said huffily. "What makes you think we'd steal any campaign ideas from you guys?"

"Because you haven't spent any time thinking about your own campaign ideas," Elizabeth retorted. "You don't have a platform, and you haven't figured out what Kimberly stands for."

"At least the kids at school know what she *doesn't* stand for. She doesn't stand for being a goody-goody, and she doesn't stand for being a tattletale."

"I did not tell on you guys," I shouted.

"Did so!" Jessica shouted back.

I couldn't believe how childish she sounded.

"Well, if you didn't tell, then Elizabeth did. She's as big a goody-goody as you are," Jessica bellowed.

"I didn't tell," Elizabeth said through gritted teeth. "But you know what?" Her eyes were narrow and hard.

"What?" Jessica snapped.

"I wish I had."

Jessica's chin jutted defiantly and she disappeared into the hall.

Why did Jessica have to ruin everything for us like that? Three minutes ago, we'd all been happy. Now we all stood around with long faces, because we felt so bad about how everyone was fighting.

Everybody said good night, and as I trooped down the stairs with the others, I wondered if it was worth it. Was any campaign really worth the heartbreak, heartache, and all-around meanness it was bringing out in us?

No. It wasn't.

I thought for a couple of seconds about dropping out of the race. But I couldn't. Not after the big speech I'd given Mandy. And not with Elizabeth, Maria, and Evie counting on me.

I guess it was about ten o'clock that night when Evie called me. I know it was late, because my mom gave me a very disapproving look when the phone rang and she answered it. "Keep it short," she whispered as she handed me the receiver.

"Hello?"

"It's Evie. And you're not going to believe what I overheard."

"What?"

"After we dropped everybody off, my grandmother and I decided we were hungry, so we stopped at Angelo's Pizza. And you know how the booths there have really high backs?"

"Uh-huh."

"Guess who came in and sat down in the booth behind us?"

"Johnny Buck?" I joked.

"I wish!" she said with a giggle. Then her tone became serious. "No, it was Kimberly and Ellen."

"Did they see you?"

"No. They didn't know I was sitting behind them, and they were talking pretty loudly. Loudly enough for me to hear every word they said." She giggled again. "Poor Grandma. Every time she tried to talk, I put my finger on my lips and shushed her so I could hear better. Guess who ratted on the kids who left campus for lunch on Thursday?"

I really hadn't given it that much thought. I just figured that some teacher had probably seen them or something. Or overheard some kids talking about it in the hall.

"Ellen Riteman," Evie said breathlessly, not even waiting for me to make a guess. "She deliberately leaked it to Mr. Clark's secretary by talking about it outside the office in a loud voice. So of course, Mrs. Knight told Mr. Clark."

"But that doesn't make any sense. Why would Ellen tell on her own friends?"

"They figured that if someone found out about their plan and all the kids got caught, it would be good publicity for Kimberly. She'd get a reputation for being brave. For being willing to stand up to Mr. Clark."

"That's the most devious thing I've ever heard," I exclaimed.

"You haven't heard all of it yet. It gets worse."

My mom came over and tapped her watch. "Hold on a minute, Evie," I said into the phone. Then I turned to my mom. "Mom, this is really important. Just one more minute?"

"All right," she said, relenting. "One minute."

I reached up and kissed my mom on the cheek. "Thanks," I said quickly. Then I put the phone back up to my mouth. "OK. I'm back. What else did you hear?"

"Only that all the time they were planning to sneak off, get caught, and make a big splash, they were planning to pin the blame on you. They figured if they could get everybody to think you were a goody-goody and a rat, nobody would vote for you."

"Of all the sneaky, low-down . . . If only you'd had a tape recorder," I said. "Then we could replay that conversation over the PA system and turn the tables on them."

"Well, I didn't have a tape recorder. So there's no way to prove that what I just said is true. But I don't think we're going to have to resort to those tactics. I think your plan stands up to Kimberly's stupid rebel reputation."

"You really think so?"

"Absolutely," Evie insisted. "All Kimberly did was get people into trouble. She didn't get the off-campus privilege back. With your plan, everybody gets to leave campus again, and nobody will wind up doing detentions for leaving campus again."

"*If* the plan gets approved," I reminded her.

"Even if it doesn't, I think it shows people that you're a thinker. And a doer. You had to pull a lot of information together fast. And you got a lot of commitments from a lot of merchants. I don't think that anything Kimberly says or does can match that."

Evie was right. And I began to feel a lot better about what was going on. It seemed almost impossible that I would lose the election. And if I won, it would prove to the other Unicorns that dirty fighting and mean behavior didn't get them anywhere. That honesty, integrity, and hard work were the qualities that people admired. Not snootiness and exclusivity.

Evie and I talked for a little while longer. It was too late to call Elizabeth and Maria by the time I got off the phone. But I could tell them everything tomorrow at school.

As I climbed the stairs to my bedroom, I felt as if a big weight had been lifted off my shoulders.

Kimberly Haver's tactics were just as pathetic as Lois Waller's. If she had to go to such elaborate lengths to make me look bad, she obviously wasn't as sure of her popularity as everyone thought

I climbed into bed and pulled the covers up to my chin. I've heard people say politics is a dirty business. Well, it might be a dirty business. But that didn't mean I couldn't run a good clean race.

There were so many things to think about that it took me a long time to fall asleep. I had the feeling that things were really about to get interesting.

"You've got to be kidding," Maria exclaimed.

Evie had just repeated the conversation she had overheard the night before for Elizabeth and Maria—word for word.

It was Monday morning, and we were standing outside in front of the school, waiting for the first bell.

Elizabeth lifted one skeptical eyebrow. "You're sure you didn't exaggerate what you heard just a little bit?"

Evie shook her head so firmly that her long curtain of dark hair swung back and forth. She lifted her hand. "Unicorn's honor. That's exactly what they said."

"How do we let people know what they did?" Maria demanded.

Elizabeth sighed heavily. "I don't think we can. It would be our word against theirs."

"Your dad's a lawyer," Maria said hopefully. "Couldn't he make them admit what they did? You know, a deposition or something?"

"I doubt it," Elizabeth said.

"Don't look so glum," I told Maria and Elizabeth. "Evie and I decided that what happened is a good sign."

Maria shook her head in confusion. "Come

again. Kimberly Haver sneaks off campus and ends up looking like a hero. She makes you look like a goody-goody. And on top of that, somebody who can't be trusted. Somebody who would rat. And this is a *good sign*?" she repeated in an incredulous voice.

"I see what she's saying," Elizabeth said thoughtfully. "Kimberly's desperate. If she can't come up with a better way to win the election than a smear campaign, it means she doesn't have any ideas. And Mary's got brilliant ideas."

"Not to mention her good looks and great personality," Maria added.

We all laughed. A long, honest laugh.

"After today, only two more days before Thursday," Evie said, looking around at each of us.

"Two more days to polish your speech," Elizabeth added.

"Two more days until you're elected president of the student council," Maria said.

*Two more days until the Unicorns shake hands and make up*, I said to myself. Or at least I hoped so.

# Thirteen

"What's this?" I asked the next morning as I sat down for breakfast. Sitting right next to my plate at the breakfast table was a big white box with a red ribbon around it.

"Just some things I ordered last week," my mom answered.

"Do I open it now or wait for Christmas?" I joked.

"Open it now," Mom instructed, pouring herself a cup of coffee.

I untied the ribbon and lifted the lid off the box. Then I began to laugh. Stacked inside the box were four straw boaters. Campaign hats. Those flat-topped white straw hats with red, white, and blue ribbons that you see people wearing at national political conventions.

"These are great!"

"Look under the hats," she instructed.

I lifted all the hats out of the box and then let out a little shriek of happiness. Under the hat was a huge stack of buttons that read "Vote for Mary Wallace!" And they had my face on them.

I jumped up and gave Mom a big hug. Up until now, I thought she hadn't realized how important all this was to me.

When you think about it, we haven't been together very long. And Mom's not a very emotional type of person. I mean, I don't know what she's thinking a lot of the time, and she doesn't know what I'm thinking. But this was so special. So supportive. So . . . *momlike.*

"Where did you get all this stuff?"

"I ordered it from a catalogue," she replied. "I thought it might be helpful." Then she took one of the buttons out of the box and pinned it proudly to the front of her dress. "Just so there's no doubt about who would get my vote," she said, and grinned.

"Hi! I'm Mary Wallace." I gave the guy coming up the steps a big grin. He was a sixth grader, so he was new to school this year. I didn't know his name, but I'd seen him around a lot. "I'm running for student council president," I said as he planted his foot on the top step.

"Uh-huh?"

"I'd really appreciate your vote on Thursday."

Another guy was coming up the front steps and heard the conversation. Before I could smile and introduce myself to him, he grabbed the first guy's arm and sort of pulled him away. "We don't vote for squealers," he said in a nasty voice.

"I didn't squeal!" I made my voice sound angry, but in control. Firm, I guess. I looked the second guy right in the eye. Didn't even blink. Just gave him a long hard stare. "And frankly," I added in a steely voice, "if you're going to fall for dirty campaign tactics like character assassination, then I don't want your votes."

I pointedly turned away from him and threw a great big smile at Sarah Thomas, who was standing a few feet away talking to Peter Burns. "Will you vote for me on Thursday?" I asked Sarah as Peter hurried away toward the science lab.

Sarah nodded. "You bet."

I reached into my backpack and pulled out one of the buttons. "Here," I said, handing it to her. "I'd appreciate a show of support."

"Can I have one of those?" a male voice asked.

It was Aaron Dallas. I was a little surprised, because I was sure he was backing Kimberly. After all, he'd been one of the people who had left campus with her. Maybe this was some mean-spirited trick. Maybe he was going to paint a mustache on my button face and wear it around school to make fun of me.

"Why do you want it?" I asked suspiciously.

"Because I think you deserve the student council seat. There's nothing like spending a whole Saturday afternoon in detention to change your political views."

I laughed and handed him a button. "Great. I'm glad you changed your mind."

"I think a lot of people's minds are changing," he said.

The two sixth-grade boys stepped forward. They were a little shy now because Aaron was there and he was older.

"You're going to vote for Mary Wallace?" the first one asked Aaron.

Aaron nodded.

The two boys looked at each other, reached a decision, then held out their hands.

I put a campaign button in each palm.

Sarah, Aaron, and the two sixth-grade boys all pinned their "Vote for Mary Wallace!" buttons onto their shirts.

"Anything else we can do?" Aaron asked.

I nodded my head. "Yes. If you hear people saying I'm a rat or a squealer, just tell them it isn't true. I never said anything to any faculty member that would have gotten anyone into trouble."

Aaron gave me the thumbs-up signal. "I believe you. Even though it seems like you're the logical person to blame, I also know you always tell the truth. And I don't think Elizabeth or Maria would be backing a rat and a squealer."

"Thanks," I said warmly. "Now if I can just convince the rest of the student body."

I'm not sure how it happened. But somehow, Kimberly's star was falling and mine was rising. Either people had forgotten about the rat rumor, or else they didn't care.

Maybe it was what Aaron had said. Maybe all the people who had wound up with detentions had become a little disenchanted with their rebel hero. Or maybe they wanted someone with a little more . . . uh, ummm, I'm not sure how to say it . . . ummmm, diplomatic ability! (That's it!) Someone who would negotiate with the faculty instead of antagonizing them.

I'm not really sure what the reason was. All I knew was that tons of people seemed to be on my side. By the end of the day, I'd given away every single button. Almost everybody I saw was wearing one. And every person I had talked to personally that day had promised to vote for me.

"I can't believe you didn't save a button for me," Elizabeth grumbled as we left campus after school that afternoon.

"I'm sorry," I apologized. "But I'll give you mine after the election. And you did get a hat."

Elizabeth reached up and tipped her hat at a passing lady. The lady laughed, and so did Elizabeth and I. "I like this hat. I may keep wearing it even after the election is over. That was really cool of your mom to get these. I think we totally outclassed the competition today."

"I'm not sure I have any competition anymore," I said. "I didn't hear a whole lot of cheers for Kimberly today."

"If Evie were here, she'd make you knock on some wood or spit between your fingers."

"Do I sound too cocky?"

"No. But my dad always says nothing's ever really in the bag until it's in the bag."

We looked at each other. "Remember Dewey," we both said in unison.

It cracked us up completely.

That's the best part of knowing Elizabeth. We're both history buffs, and we both love to read. So we always get each other's jokes.

We were on our way to the stationery store to get some more poster board. I thought I'd make a couple of "Vote for Mary Wallace" signs to hang in the cafeteria.

We were just passing the little grocery store next to the stationery shop when Mrs. Willard came hurrying out, practically bumping right into us.

"Hi, Mrs. Willard," we both chorused.

Mrs. Willard smiled. "How are you girls?"

We both rolled our eyes dramatically and let our shoulders slump. If only she knew.

"Running for office is a lot of work," Mrs. Willard said.

"Harder than we thought," Elizabeth answered.

"We miss you girls at the Center," she said. "The children ask about you constantly. We do have a few volunteers helping us out, but the sooner you can get back on your regular schedule, the better."

"We will," I promised.

"Will you tell the other girls, too?"

Elizabeth and I exchanged an uneasy look.

I opened my mouth, but before I could say anything, Elizabeth spoke up. "We can't speak for all the other girls. To be honest, we're not on very friendly terms with some of them right now. And we won't be at least until the election is over."

Mrs. Willard frowned thoughtfully. "I don't care what kind of squabbles you girls get into amongst yourselves. That's your business. But my business is the children. They depend on you to come. And when you don't, no matter how good an explanation you give them, you're just not being fair to them."

"The election is over Thursday," Elizabeth said softly. "We'll come Thursday afternoon."

"Can I regard that as a promise?" Mrs. Willard asked.

We both nodded.

She shot a look at our campaign hats. "Win or lose?"

We both nodded again.

"Fine." Then her face broke into a smile. "Good luck," she said to Mary. "I think you'll make a very fine student council president."

Then she turned and walked quickly toward her car, which was parked along the curb.

"I feel just awful about how we've ignored the kids at the Center," I said. "I haven't even given them a second thought in the last couple of days."

Elizabeth lifted her campaign hat and scratched the top of her head. "Me, either."

"This makes us as bad as the Unicorns," I said.

There was a long silence. Then she said softly, "We *are* the Unicorns."

I looked at Elizabeth and she looked at me.

My mouth fell open. I couldn't believe what I'd just said. It was like Kimberly and her crowd were the Unicorns, and we were another club altogether.

I mentally replayed my conversation with Mandy. I'd convinced her, and myself, that this was a temporary fight. But somehow, it didn't seem as temporary anymore.

"Still think things will really get back to normal after the election?" Elizabeth asked tentatively.

"I hope so," I said. "Not just for the sake of the kids at the center but for everyone's sake. Especially Mandy's. I think this is harder on her than it is on any of us."

Poor Mandy. She was torn absolutely in two. Not sure about who we all were or where she fit in. She was totally confused.

*Her and me both*, I thought unhappily as we walked into the stationery shop.

Jessica. Lila. Ellen. They had all been my friends.

Good friends. We'd been friends all through last year. Had fights. Made up. Argued with one another. Cried with one another. Laughed at one another's jokes.

I didn't want to lose those friendships. Not if I could help it. But they had pushed me away. Started fighting dirty. Made everything personal.

After the election, could we pick up where we had left off? Forgive and forget all the ugly things that had been said?

I began to wish this whole thing had never gotten started. I wished that there had been some way I could have stayed neutral, like Mandy.

"Look at this," Elizabeth said, holding up a piece of poster board. "It's a little thicker than the other board, and it doesn't cost any more. I say let's use this."

I walked over to the end of the aisle, where Elizabeth was looking at the different kinds of poster board.

"The only problem is they don't have it in dead white. Just cream," she continued. "And I think big black letters on dead-white poster board would be easier to read."

It was then that I caught a glimpse of a familiar figure way over on the other side of the aisle.

It was Mandy. And she wasn't alone. I tugged on Elizabeth's sleeve. "Look over there," I whispered.

Elizabeth's eyes darted in the direction of my

pointing finger, and she let out a little gasp.

Right next to Mandy's elbow stood Kimberly. Kimberly looked as though she was talking a mile a minute. Lips moving. Hands gesturing. Every once in a while, Mandy would throw back her head and laugh.

They moved slowly along the aisle—Mandy's eyes were searching the shelves for something. Kimberly moved right along with her.

Mandy came to a sudden stop, as if she had located what she was looking for.

"Come on," Elizabeth whispered. "Let's get closer."

Elizabeth and I moved over one aisle just in time to see Mandy remove something from the shelf and hand it to Kimberly. It was a package of letter stencils.

"These will make a poster look really professional," we heard her say to Kimberly.

"Thanks, Mandy," Kimberly said. "You're a real friend."

Mandy nodded as Kimberly hurried up to the cash register to pay for her purchase.

"I don't think this is as hard on Mandy as you thought," Elizabeth whispered.

"I think you're right," I whispered back.

Elizabeth and I walked down the aisle toward Mandy. Mandy turned suddenly, saw us, and took a step backward, as if she was about to run away.

"I thought you weren't taking sides," I said in a dry tone.

"I'm not," she answered evenly.

I could feel an angry flush rising up my neck and creeping onto my cheeks. "In my book, aiding and abetting the enemy is the same thing as taking a side."

Mandy's eyes flashed angrily, and this time she stepped forward, not backward. "Enemy!" she repeated in an outraged voice. "Since when did Kimberly become your *enemy*?"

"I guess when she turned you against me," I practically yelled.

"Nobody's turned me against anybody," she insisted in a loud voice. "She asked me for advice. Advice about making posters. I gave it to her. If you had asked me for advice, I would have given it to you, too."

With that, Mandy turned on her heel and stalked away. My heart was pounding, I was so mad and upset. I didn't know what to think about Mandy anymore. I didn't know what to think about Kimberly, or the club, or the election, or anything.

# Fourteen

"So in conclusion, I'd just like to remind you that—"

"Stop!" Elizabeth shouted in a frustrated voice.

I lifted my eyes from the three-page speech I was practicing. "What's the matter now?"

"You're still just reading it in a monotone. I don't hear any enthusiasm."

"I don't feel very enthusiastic," I replied.

Elizabeth sat down on the edge of her bed and dropped her head in her hands. "If this is what real politics is like, I'm not even going to register to vote. You're making me feel as depressed as you look."

"Well, after all that's happened, how am I supposed to look?" I snapped.

"Like you at least believe in what you're saying," she snapped back. "I worked hard on that speech. The least you can do is pretend you care about the things you're saying.

"Well, *excuse me*, Madame Pulitzer," I said sarcastically.

Elizabeth and I stared daggers at each other for a couple of seconds. Then I felt the anger drain out of me like air out of a balloon. "I'm really sorry."

"Me, too," she said immediately.

I sat down on the edge of the bed. "It's just hard to feel enthusiastic. I don't know why."

"Because no matter who wins tomorrow, we've lost all the important things," Elizabeth answered. "Our camaraderie. Our faith in one another. Our ability to bring out the good qualities in one another."

"Do you think we've lost those things *forever*?" I asked in a whisper.

Elizabeth just shook her head in uncertainty. "I wish I knew." She stood up and briskly dusted her hands together. "Let's not dwell on it, OK? Let's just throw ourselves at Job One. Learning the speech and delivering it with gusto. Tomorrow's the big day."

"I'm not sure I can do that," I said with a sigh. "I'm not good at memorizing stuff. I'm not even sure I can hold up this speech to read. My hands shake like crazy when I'm nervous. And I'm so incredibly nervous, there's a good possibility that I might just get up on that stage tomorrow, say hello, and then throw up all over the first row."

Elizabeth let out a big laugh. "Remind me to find a seat safely in the back."

That made me laugh, and being able to laugh made me feel more relaxed.

"You're right. If you're holding the paper, people will see your hands shaking. And that's not good."

"What's the alternative?"

Elizabeth went over to the fern stand in the corner of the room. It was tall, with a pedestal shape. She put the fern on the floor and then moved the stand to the middle of the room. "Pretend this is a podium. Now watch what I'm doing."

She laid the speech on top of the "podium." Then she leaned forward slightly and rested her hands on either side. "Now, remember, the top of the podium is slanted slightly toward you. So the audience can't see what's on it. Are you following me?"

I nodded and she went on. "I'll use a highlighter on the opening sentence of each paragraph. That way, you can just put the pages down in front of you, and very casually glance down occasionally to cue you on where you are and what to say."

"That's a great idea," I said, relieved. "And I think it will work out fine."

Elizabeth smiled. "Do we still need to post barf warnings on the front row?"

"I hope not."

Elizabeth reached back and tightened her blond ponytail with an efficient air. "Let me start highlighting. Then you can take another crack at reading it."

I nodded. "I'll be with you in two minutes. But first, I need to use your bathroom."

Elizabeth gestured toward the bathroom with an exaggerated bow and grand sweep of her arm. "Madame, it's all yours."

I was still giggling as I went into the blue-and-white bathroom that Elizabeth and Jessica shared and shut the door.

Jessica must not have been around that day, because the bathroom was neat as a pin. No water on the counter. No rumpled towels stuffed into the towel racks. No makeup tissues littering the floor.

I could hear Elizabeth congratulating herself in her room. "This is a good speech, even if I do say so myself," I heard her mutter.

After I'd finished, I washed my hands and dried them on one of the neatly folded blue towels. I refolded the towel and hung it back on the rack. Then I wiped up the little bit of water that I'd splashed on the counter when I washed my hands.

When I was satisfied that the bathroom was as neat and clean as I had found it, I went back into Elizabeth's room. "OK," I said as enthusiastically as I could. "Let's do it."

An hour and a half later, Elizabeth gave me an encouraging nod and then motioned with her hands like a symphony conductor telling the string section to snap it up. "Project!" she reminded me in a soft voice. "Project."

"So in conclusion . . ." I said in a louder voice.

"That's it," Elizabeth interjected. "You want the back row to hear you."

". . . I'd like to simply say that I have already demonstrated my commitment to the concerns of the Sweet Valley student body, and if I am elected, you can depend on me to continue working on your behalf."

"Bravo!" Elizabeth shouted, jumping to her feet. "You did it. You did a great job."

"Could you tell that I had to refer to my notes about every two seconds?" I asked nervously.

Elizabeth shook her head. "No. You were really subtle. So don't worry about that." She took the speech from my hand. "So now, it's back into the drawer."

"Don't you think I should take it home with me tonight so I can practice more?"

"No. I think if you keep going over it and over it, you'll be stale on it by tomorrow. I'll bring it to school with me in the morning and give it to you just before assembly. In the meantime, you try to relax, get a good night's sleep, and don't worry."

I looked at my watch. "Wow! It's late. I'd better get home before I get into trouble."

"Need to call your mom?"

"No. I've got my bike." I reached for my Unicorn jacket, which was lying on Elizabeth's bed.

Then I put it back down. It was a long ride home. It was probably a good idea to use Elizabeth's bathroom again.

While Elizabeth put the speech away and turned off her computer, I went into the bathroom again. As I opened the door, I gasped.

It was hard to believe it was the same bathroom I'd been in before. It was an absolute mess.

There was water all over the counter. The towels were lying on the floor. And a dozen different eye shadow and lip gloss tubes were strewn across the white Formica counter.

What in the world had happened?

Then I heard Jessica's voice as she talked on the phone out in the hallway. I smiled crookedly into the mirror. It didn't take Amanda Howard (our favorite fictional detective) to figure out what had happened. Hurricane Jessica had been in here.

I began to pick up the towels and refold them. Elizabeth had done a lot for me today. The least I could do was clean up her bathroom.

It didn't take long. And by the time I walked out, it looked neat as a pin again.

Elizabeth gave me a big smile. "I don't think you can lose," she said.

Then we both knocked on wood and pretended to spit through our fingers.

# Fifteen

I woke up on Thursday morning with a huge, heavy lump in my stomach. And when I say huge, I'm talking super huge. Gigunda-sized. A mondo-lump. Right below my ribs.

I was so groggy, I couldn't remember what was making me feel so awful. Then my eyes flew open and I sat up straight. "Today is election day!"

*Boom!* went my feet as I jumped out of bed and hit the floor running. I was supposed to meet Elizabeth just before the morning assembly to get my speech.

Just as she had instructed, I'd done my best not to think about it anymore last night. But as I brushed my teeth and washed my face and put on my clothes for school, I wondered if it wouldn't have been better to bring it home and memorize it.

Oh, sure, I had little bits and pieces of it committed to memory. But I was going to really be relying on the typed copy and the highlighted cues at the beginning of each paragraph.

The lump was still there when I went down to breakfast.

"Good morning," Mom said in a cheerful voice.

"Good morning," I answered flatly, sitting down at the breakfast table.

"Ready for the big day?"

I took a deep breath and moved around a little in my seat—just to check if the lump was still there.

It was.

I wondered if all politicians felt that way before an election. "I'm as ready as I'll ever be," I responded. "But I feel really nervous."

"You'll feel better after breakfast," Mom promised. She came over and put a big steaming bowl of oatmeal in front of me.

Uggghhhh! No way could I get that down.

Add a little oatmeal, and that lump was going to turn from a mondolump into a megamondolump.

I got up and found the bread. "I think I'll just have a piece of toast this morning."

Mom looked concerned. "Are you feeling all right? You usually have a big appetite for breakfast."

"Not today," I said. "My stomach feels heavy."

I put a piece of toast in the toaster and then sat back down, waiting for it to pop up. Mom sat down in the chair next to mine and took my hand.

"Mary. It's just a school election. If you lose, it doesn't matter. There are a million events and clubs and opportunities in your future. So please, if you lose this election, promise me you won't feel as if it's ruined your entire life."

"Mom?" I said softly when she was through talking.

"Yes, dear?"

"Do we have any heartburn medicine in the house?"

I'd been waiting at the front door of the school for what seemed like an hour. Kids had been streaming past me for the last ten minutes.

A lot of them had stopped to wish me luck. But it wasn't luck I needed. It was my speech.

My heart sort of turned over and sank to the pit of my stomach when I saw Kimberly coming up the stairs with Jessica, Ellen, and Lila behind her.

They all had smug smiles on their faces, and they were actually swaggering. They looked so self-confident, it was demoralizing. *Chill out, Mary,* I said to myself in a stern tone. *You've got a solid platform to run on, and all Kimberly's got is a reputation for getting kids into trouble.*

"You've got my vote," said a voice at my elbow just as Kimberly and company got up to the front doors.

I looked over and saw Randy Mason staring solemnly at me through his thick glasses.

"But you haven't heard my speech yet," I said.

He shook his head. "All I know is that Kimberly got a bunch of kids in trouble and you didn't."

I smiled, but then . . .

"Oooohh, Kimberly," Lila said in mock fear. "Look out. Mary's got the geek vote all sewn up."

Ellen and Jessica began to giggle, and I could feel my face turning bright red. "You know what?" I responded angrily. "With an opponent like you, I probably didn't even need to campaign for this office. All I have to do is wait for you to lose the race all by yourself by insulting the voters."

Kimberly turned up the corner of her mouth and made a little marking motion in the air. "Two points," she said to me in mock approval. "Very good."

Then her eyebrows snapped together and her mouth formed a grim line. "But you'll need a whole lot more than two points to beat me in this election."

"I'll get them," I said, looking directly into her eyes.

Kimberly's face relaxed into its customary smug smile. "What would you think about a little bet?"

I felt beads of perspiration forming on my upper lip. Where was Maria? Where was Evie? Where was Elizabeth? *And where was my speech?*

I glanced at my watch. They were all fifteen minutes late.

"You haven't answered my question," Kimberly reminded me.

"What kind of a bet?" I asked warily.

"If we win, we get your Unicorn jackets," she

said with a sneer. "If you win, you get ours."

I furrowed my brow. "What do you mean?" I asked slowly.

"What do you think I mean?" she answered hotly.

Was she telling me they were a separate club now? Forever and always? That win or lose, only half of us would be Unicorns after today?

I saw Elizabeth, Maria, and Evie running toward us.

"Is it a bet," Kimberly whispered urgently into my ear, "or don't you think the goody-goodies can win?"

I looked at Elizabeth's face and remembered how hard she had worked on my speech. I looked at Maria and remembered all her wise words and kind advice. I looked at Evie and saw how young and eager she was. What would she think if I backed down from a challenge like this?

"It's a bet," I answered quietly.

Kimberly and her crew melted into the crowd and disappeared just as Elizabeth, Maria, and Evie hit the top step.

The minute I saw Elizabeth's face I knew something was wrong.

"What is it?" I asked.

Elizabeth was breathing so hard from running, she could hardly talk. "Your speech," she gasped. "I can't find it."

"*What!*"

"I can't find your speech," Elizabeth repeated, and her voice sounded as if she was close to tears.

"I can't find the printout. And the computer disk is gone, too."

*Sproinnggg!* went that little spring in my stomach. It was a strange sensation, but I knew what it meant. It meant I had just gone from slightly nervous to full-scale panic. Zero to sixty-five on the emotional speedometer. I grabbed Elizabeth by the shoulders. "You can't have lost my speech," I insisted in a loud voice.

"I took it out last night, to make a few minor changes, and then"—Elizabeth's face was white and she was wringing her hands in despair—"I put it back in the drawer. But this morning when I went to get it, it was gone."

"We all searched her room," Maria said in a grim voice.

"This is nuts!" I cried.

The final bell was ringing now. We had no choice but to go inside.

"Come on," Evie urged. "If we hurry, maybe we can still get seats together."

My heart was pounding. My legs were shaking. And I couldn't stop clenching and unclenching my fists. We were all sitting in assembly, and Mr. Clark was up at the podium making his usual speech about the importance of student government.

Elizabeth was sitting on my right, and Maria was sitting on my left. Both of them kept whispering to each other across my lap.

Elizabeth was wildly scrawling out some notes for me on some sheets of paper that she had ripped out of her notebook. "It's not much, but this will keep you from getting up there and freezing."

"Shhhh," said a boy in the row behind us.

Elizabeth dropped her voice a little lower. "Here's your first sentence: 'I'm not here to talk about what I promise to do. I'm here to tell you what I've already done.' That should cue you on your opening paragraph."

I nodded, watching her as she wrote out a few more key phrases and then, finally, the part that said: "I have secured the financial commitment of the entire Merchants' Association. Now all that remains to be done is secure the permission of the PTA and the school district." Then it ended with the part about my having demonstrated my commitment to the concerns of the students of Sweet Valley Middle School.

"This should get you through," Elizabeth said confidently. "Lots of it is coming back to me, and it will to you, too."

"Our first speaker and candidate for student council president," Mr. Clark was saying now, "is Kimberly Haver."

There was a loud burst of applause, and Kimberly came confidently up the aisle with a smile on her face. When she climbed the steps to the podium, a couple of the boys actually cheered.

Kimberly smiled out over the audience and then made a motion like she was applauding the audience. "Thank you for that welcome," she said into the mike. "I can't tell you how glad I am to be back. And how glad I am to have the honor of running for the office of president of the Sweet Valley Middle School student council."

The audience was quiet now.

Kimberly cleared her throat, moved her papers around a bit on the podium, and then leaned forward, resting her hands on either side of the podium.

*Darn*, I thought, casting my eyes downward to review my notes. *There goes my hand gesture.*

"First of all," Kimberly said. "I'm not going to get up here and tell you what I promise to do. I'm going to tell you what I've already done."

My head came up like a shot, and Maria and Elizabeth's heads snapped toward me so fast I practically heard a cracking noise.

"That's your speech!" Maria squeaked in horror. "How did Kimberly manage to steal your speech?"

Elizabeth gasped. "Kimberly didn't steal it," she whispered as she slowly realized what had happened. "Jessica did. She stole it and gave it to Kimberly."

"But how?" Maria practically moaned.

Elizabeth shook her head in confusion as Kimberly's voice went on and on, rising and falling as she delivered a string of familiar phrases.

Last night, when I'd gone into the bathroom at the Wakefields' that second time, it had been a mess. The way I had figured things, Jessica had been in there and had overheard us talking. Overheard my speech. And somehow she had discovered Elizabeth's secret hiding place.

There was a tap on my shoulder, and I looked behind me and saw Jessica smirk. "All's fair in love, war, and school elections." Then she leaned back in her seat and held out her hands, palms up, so that Lila and Ellen could each slap the hands. They all slumped arrogantly down into their seats, and Ellen actually blew a bubble with her gum and popped it with a loud *smack*.

"So in conclusion . . ." Kimberly was saying in a louder voice, "I'd like to simply say that I have already demonstrated my commitment to the concerns of the Sweet Valley student body, and if elected, you can depend on me to continue working on your behalf."

*"Hooray!"* shouted several people. Then, as one, the audience leapt to its feet, and Kimberly smiled, acknowledging the wild burst of applause. My hands were clutching the arms of my chair so tightly that my knuckles were white.

Kimberly was stepping down now, descending the little flight of steps that led up to the stage. Then she came up the aisle. As she walked by our row, she met my eye briefly and winked.

"Our next candidate and speaker," boomed Mr. Clark's voice through the mike, "is Mary Wallace."

# Sixteen

I felt Maria and Elizabeth's fingers prying my own fingers off the arm of my chair.

"It's your turn to speak," Maria urged.

"Kimberly stole my speech," I hissed in hysteria. "Go tell Mr. Clark I withdraw."

"No way!" both Elizabeth and Maria said in unison.

"I can't do it," I insisted. "I can't get up there cold and think of something to say."

"Just fake it. Don't worry about the election anymore. That's gone. Just try to get through the speech."

I shook my head. "I can't. I just can't."

"You have to at least try," Elizabeth insisted. "You can't just give up without trying to put up some kind of fight."

"Think of your friends," Maria whispered. "Of what we've all been through these last weeks. It will all have been for nothing if you take the coward's way out."

They were right. I leaned forward a little and saw Evie's long curtain of hair framing her concerned face. Evie looked up to us so much. Maria was right. I had to set an example.

"But what will I say?" I asked tearfully. "What will I do?"

"Wing it," Elizabeth commanded. "You can do it."

Maria and Elizabeth both hoisted me to my feet.

"Library books," Maria whispered behind me as I made my way up to the stage on shaking legs.

"Extra credit," Elizabeth added.

I don't know how I actually got my legs to cooperate well enough to get them to climb the short staircase up to the stage. But somehow, I did.

I got to the podium, adjusted the microphone, and then thrust my hands down into the front pockets of my pants so that no one could see them shake.

"As you all know," I began, "I'm Mary Wallace . . ."

*Why did my voice sound so high and tinny?*

". . . and I'm running for president of the student council."

"Well, duh!" said somebody in the front row.

The whole front row began to snicker. I scanned the auditorium. All I saw was row after row after row of bored and uninterested faces. Kimberly had held their interest by talking about an exciting subject—leaving campus.

It was a tough act to follow. Library books and extra-credit projects were not going to get and keep their interest. But what choice did I have?

I took a deep breath and began to speak. "I'd like to talk about the situation in the library," I said in a breathy voice. "Right now, we have a four-book limit. I think the limit should be raised. Lengthy research projects usually demand more resource material, and . . ."

I was interrupted by a loud snore from the back of the auditorium. The entire room seemed to be giggling and snickering.

I rattled on a little more about the library's checkout policy, my voice getting shakier and shakier until I could barely talk above a whisper.

"We can't hear you in the back!" an antagonistic male voice shouted.

"Yeah! Speak up!" another voice rang out.

I swallowed hard and saw Elizabeth's face.

"Project," she was mouthing. "Project."

Behind her I saw Lila, Ellen, Kimberly, and Jessica all laughing and elbowing each other.

And way in the back of the auditorium, sitting perfectly still with her eyes cast downward, was Mandy.

"So in conclusion," I said as loudly as I could, "I would . . . just like to ask for your vote as well as your confidence."

There. I'd done it. Gotten up in front of the audience and somehow muddled my way through.

But half the faces in the audience looked asleep. And the other half looked as if they were sneering.

Suddenly, the lump in my throat reappeared, and even though my mouth was open and working, no sounds were coming out.

There was a horrible aching feeling in my stomach and my chest. I looked down at the podium and saw the steady *drip, drip drip* of my tears splattering down.

There was some scattered applause as I turned and ran behind the curtain, cut across the stage, dodging pieces of old theater department scenery, and raced down the backstage steps into the hall.

There was nobody there. My mind was racing. I'd just made a complete fool out of myself. Where could I go? Where could I hide?

Then I remembered the library. There were four private carrels where the doors could be shut. They were usually used by study groups before exams.

I hurried down the hall toward the library, took a right, and found an empty carrel. I shut the door and pushed the little button in the knob that made it lock.

I sat down and stared at the white wall for what seemed like an hour. And then I burst into tears all over again.

*Knock, knock!*
I didn't answer. I was still huddled in the corner

of the carrel. I'd skipped my morning classes. No way could I let myself be seen. Some people look appealingly vulnerable when they cry. Not me. My nose swells until it looks like a potato. My eyes turn into two bloodshot squints. And my lips? Bleghh! They look like two pieces of liver.

*Knock, knock!* I heard again.

"This carrel is occupied," I said in a thick voice.

"We know it's occupied," said a familiar voice impatiently. "Now would you please let us in."

I got up, peeped through the door, and saw Evie, Maria, and Elizabeth standing on the other side.

"What do you want?" I was feeling so victimized and persecuted, I thought everybody was my enemy. Even my friends.

"Please let us in," Elizabeth pleaded softly.

Even though I didn't feel like talking to anybody, I opened the door and let them in.

Maria and Evie leaned against the wall with their arms across their chests, and Elizabeth and I sat down in the chairs.

"They counted the ballots," Maria said.

"And?" I asked.

Evie rolled her eyes and flipped the hair off of her shoulders. "Kimberly Haver is the winner."

"By a landslide," Elizabeth said softly.

"How do we fight back on this?" Evie demanded in a frustrated tone.

"I don't think we can," Maria said unhappily. "Kimberly presented the plan as her own. It's all ready to go, pending approval from the PTA and the faculty. In about another ten minutes, nobody will remember or care whose plan it was. All they'll care about is that the off-campus privilege will be reinstated."

"I can't believe they would do this to me," I moaned. "Those girls were my *friends*."

"With friends like that . . ." Maria shook her head.

"I can't believe my own sister would do something like this to me," Elizabeth said softly.

"Oh, Elizabeth," I croaked. "What happened? We were all so tight. As tight as you and Jessica. Now look at us."

"We're different people, I guess," Elizabeth breathed. "But you know what?" she added in a steely tone. "I wouldn't want to be like them for a million dollars."

"This is a sad moment," Evie commented.

"I think that's what's called a masterpiece of understatement," Maria commented dryly.

"Why don't we tell Mr. Clark?" Evie asked.

We all held a silent conversation, everyone's eyes scanning the other faces. Every face expressed the same opinion with a flat, nonsmiling look.

Maria shrugged finally. "Like Mary said—over and over—we're not squealers. There will be other elections. Other chances to even the score. We'll just have to wait."

A bell rang. "Let's move out," Maria said briskly. "We can't hide in here all day."

"Maybe you can't," I said angrily. "But I can." I pointed to my face, and Maria winced a little.

"You've got a point. You don't exactly look like a gracious loser."

"I'm going to hide out here until the middle of the next class, then I'm sneaking out and going home. Why don't you guys meet me at my house tonight? Around seven?"

"You'll get in trouble for missing classes," Evie protested.

"I've already missed all my heavy classes. All I have in the afternoon is P.E. and a study hall," I replied.

Reluctantly, the other girls left the room.

"I hate leaving you like this," Elizabeth said.

"Don't worry." I tried to smile. "I'd really rather be alone for now."

"I feel like it's my fault," Elizabeth blurted out. "I wasn't careful enough. I wasn't—"

Like lightning, I interrupted her. "It wasn't your fault," I insisted. "It wasn't anybody's fault. They cheated. That's all there is to it. They're total scum and they cheated."

By the time everybody showed up that night, I was a lot calmer. I told Mom and Tim what had happened. Tim was so upset and unhappy for me, it was all I could do to keep him from charging over to Kimberly Haver's house and giving her father an earful.

Luckily, Mom and I were able to talk him out of that.

Knowing what happened made them both more sympathetic than they might have otherwise been when I told them I had skipped a bunch of classes that day—because I had been so upset and everything.

"Well, of course you couldn't go to class under those conditions," Mom said, hugging me as tightly as she could.

"Thanks, Mom. I'm glad you understand."

Then I told her that my friends were coming over that evening for a meeting. Mom didn't waste a second. Five minutes later, she was in the kitchen changing the lettering on the victory cake she had made. Instead of "Congratulations, Mary," it now read "We Love You, Mary."

Having so much support at home made it easier to open the door and smile when Maria, Evie, and Elizabeth arrived. "Come in," I invited them.

"Wow!" Maria said sadly, looking around the dining room. "You look like you were all ready for a victory party."

"We were," Mom said, hurrying in with a fresh plate of cookies. "But now we've decided it's a party in honor of friendship, loyalty, and honesty."

We each picked up a cup of punch. "To friendship, loyalty, and honesty," we all said solemnly. But before we could put the cups to our lips, the doorbell rang.

"I'll get it," Mom said, hurrying out of the little dining room.

A few moments later, she reappeared. Following her into the room was Mandy!

Nobody said anything for a long, long time. But nobody could miss the fact that she was wearing a Unicorn jacket. We had all put our jackets in a big box to turn over to Kimberly tomorrow. We'd lost them in the bet. But it didn't matter. We all agreed that we didn't want them anymore.

My mother must have felt the tension in the room, so she excused herself immediately. "I'll let you girls talk amongst yourselves," she said with an understanding smile. Then she went into the kitchen and shut the door behind her.

"I know what happened," Mandy said.

"How?"

"I was just over at Kimberly Haver's house. They were having a party. They . . . they . . ." Mandy swallowed hard, as if she were having a hard time speaking. "They were *bragging* about it," she finally blurted out.

I put my cup down. "So?"

Mandy's eyelashes fluttered down. "What do you mean, 'So?'" she asked softly.

"So what are you going to do about it?" I demanded.

"I don't know," Mandy wailed. She threw herself into a chair and put her head down on her folded-up arms.

"I can't believe you, Mandy Miller," I said angrily. "Right is right and wrong is wrong. I know that sometimes what's right and what's wrong just depends on your point of view. But in this case, the choice is so clear."

Mandy lifted her head. "Look, I didn't sign on to be judge and jury of Kimberly Haver. I signed on to be the president of the Unicorns. President of a club." Her eyes narrowed. "You were the one who told me to keep on believing in the club. Remember? You were the one who said that we would see everybody's good qualities come out after the election."

"I said they'd come out *if I won*," I reminded her. "Mandy, I want us all to be friends, too. But it's not happening. I don't know if it ever will. If this club ever is going to work, we all have to play by the same rules. A code of ethics only works if everybody abides by it."

I looked around for help, but the others had backed up against the wall. Withdrawn somehow. That made it clear that this was between Mandy and me.

I knelt down beside Mandy and put my hand on hers. I felt sorry for her. I really did. She had tried so hard to stay above everything, but we'd dragged her into it anyway.

"You have to pick a side, Mandy," I said softly.

"But they're my friends, too," she sobbed. "Right or wrong, they're my friends, too."

I shook my head. "After everything they've done, they're still your friends? They cheated, they lied, they stole—and you're so loyal, you still think of them as friends? Well, I don't." I took a deep breath as everything just came spilling out. "I may be a goody-goody, and that's just fine. I like being good. Being fair. Playing by the rules. I like knowing I've tried hard to think of other people's feelings, to be responsible, to do what's right. I used to think you felt the same way."

Mandy's shoulders shook, and she stood, looking around. Then she let out a great big sob and went plunging toward the front door.

For a long moment, nobody said a word. I went over to the table and picked up my punch glass, determined not to let Mandy's visit spoil our party. "To friendship, loyalty, and honesty," I said.

The tension in the room slowly began to disappear, and Evie even smiled as she picked up her own cup.

Elizabeth and Maria did the same.

"To friendship, loyalty, and honesty," they all echoed. Then we clinked our glasses.

# Seventeen

I just barely got to school on time the next morning. And it took forever to get there, hauling my books and the big box of jackets I was supposed to turn over to Kimberly.

The box full of jackets wouldn't fit into my locker. Maria's locker is near mine, and I was just thinking of looking for her and asking her to store some of the jackets when I heard three sharp buzzing sounds. That meant there was going to be a surprise assembly.

Suddenly, the great wave of students that had been surging away from the lockers toward the classrooms came surging back in the other direction toward the auditorium. I had to practically paste myself and the box against the wall to keep from getting knocked over.

As the whole herd thundered by, I caught a glimpse of Maria. She pushed and shouldered her way through the crowd in my direction, then waited a few moments with me until the crowd thinned out enough for us to join in the migration.

"Any idea what this is about?" Maria asked.

"None," I responded.

When we entered the auditorium, we immediately saw Elizabeth and Evie sitting in a row toward the back. They waved us over, pointing to the two seats they had saved for us.

Little by little, we inched our way to our seats.

"What's with the box?" Evie asked.

"Our jackets. I haven't seen Kimberly yet," I replied curtly. "Keep an eye out for her. They won't fit in my locker, so maybe I'll just hand them over after this assembly. Let it be their problem."

Elizabeth made a wry face and Evie glowered. "Ohhhhh, I just wish there were some way to get them back."

"That makes two of us," Maria echoed softly.

"That makes three of us," Elizabeth said grimly.

"Hey, hey!" I cautioned. "We're the good guys. Remember?"

"How can I forget," Maria grumbled, "when everywhere I go I hear people calling me 'goody-goody' behind my back?"

After that, there was no more time for discussion, because Mr. Clark got up on the podium and rapped on it for order.

The excited babble in the auditorium faded into a dull hum, which then drifted into absolute silence.

Mr. Clark looked out over the audience for a long time. He cleared his throat and knitted his brow. Then he appeared to be thinking some more.

Everybody around me began to shift nervously in their seat.

Finally, Mr. Clark leaned toward the mike. "I have been informed that the popular compromise regarding the restoration of off-campus lunch privileges that was presented yesterday was not the work of Kimberly Haver." Everyone gasped. "It was really the work of Mary Wallace. Her campaign speech was stolen by the opposition."

Mr. Clark took off his glasses and let out a weary sigh. "Stealing work and passing it off as your own is an unconscionable act. Frankly, I cannot find words strong enough to express my outrage. And unfortunately, our national elections do not set a standard of honesty or integrity for our young people to emulate."

He looked all around the room again. And he seemed upset. "The world is certainly not a very moral place these days. But I would have hoped that the persons involved in this incident would have displayed a little more sense. They will be dealt with—and severely."

Everybody was so astonished by what Mr. Clark was saying, they were absolutely silent.

"Under the circumstances, I'm calling for a second

election. You will have fifteen minutes to consider your choice, then you may cast your ballots as you file out. Now, I know that very often, these elections turn into popularity contests. And I know that I can't tell you how to vote. But I do ask you to think very carefully before you vote. The results of this election, right or wrong, will stand. That is all."

We all sat there with our mouths open.

Mr. Clark quickly veered back toward the microphone. "Will Ms. Wallace and Ms. Haver report to my office immediately, please, to await the results of the election?"

I slapped my hand down on Elizabeth's knee and stood. "I don't know how you did this, but I hope it works."

"I didn't do anything," Elizabeth said, sounding surprised. "We all agreed not to tell. I don't know how he found out."

"Hang on to these until I get back, OK?" I said, shoving the big box of jackets toward Maria.

"You got it," she replied.

There was a lot of murmuring and staring as Kimberly and I made our way up the aisles to the back doors of the auditorium.

On our way out, I heard Ms. Luster, our librarian, giving the voting instructions. "Please use half of a notebook-sized sheet of paper, write the name of your candidate on it, and fold it in half. Then drop it in the ballot boxes that are located on either side of the front entrances."

"Squealer," I heard Kimberly hiss behind me.

I turned so quickly, it forced her to bump into me. So there we were. Nose to nose. Eye to eye. "I didn't squeal," I said through gritted teeth. "But maybe you should ask Ellen if *she* leaked this story to Mr. Clark's secretary along with the plans for sneaking off campus."

"How did you know about that?" Kimberly gasped angrily.

I didn't answer. I wasn't about to say I'd gotten that information from an eavesdropper. As I marched on down the hall toward Mr. Clark's office, I couldn't help smiling. That was another couple of points for me.

I couldn't help wondering, too, how Mr. Clark had found out about the stolen speech—unless Ellen really had gotten another case of the blabs outside Mr. Clark's office.

"Will you please sit down, girls." Mr. Clark's secretary, Mrs. Knight, pointed to two hard-backed chairs, one on either side of the room.

Her words were phrased as if she were making a request, but no doubt about it, it was an order.

Immediately, Kimberly took one chair and I took the other. Since there were no magazines around to look at, we were sort of forced to stare at each other.

Mrs. Knight turned her back to us and began to type, and Kimberly didn't waste a second before she began to taunt me. "Goody-goody," she mouthed. Then she twisted her lips into a parody of prissiness and pretended to dust a speck of lint off her blouse.

I didn't respond. Why play her game? But I did roll my eyes.

Mrs. Knight turned quickly and caught a glimpse of Kimberly's face. "Are you ill?" She shot the question at Kimberly like a drill sergeant.

"Uh . . . nooo," Kimberly said in confusion. She began to cough elaborately. "I just got something stuck in my throat."

Mrs. Knight motioned toward the water cooler, which was just over my shoulder. "You may get a drink over there."

Kimberly got up, took a little cone-shaped cup out of the dispenser, filled it with water, put it to her mouth, and then, with a deft movement of her hand, managed to pour the ice cold water into my lap.

"Ayyyiii," I screamed in surprise, jumping to my feet.

"Ms. Wallace," Mrs. Knight rumbled. "What is the meaning of this outburst?"

I glared daggers at Kimberly, whose face was completely bland. "Goody-goody rat," she mouthed again.

She had me. I couldn't tell on her without being a goody-goody or a rat or a squealer. "Ahhhh," I said, thinking fast, "I just had a cramp in my leg."

I bent my leg back and forth, as if trying to

stretch it. And as Kimberly started back to her seat, I quickly stretched out my leg and . . .

*Blam!*

Kimberly hit the floor like a ton of bricks.

"Ms. Haver," Mrs. Knight said in exasperation. "What is the matter now?"

"I just . . . uh, tripped over my shoelace," Kimberly said lamely.

Boy! If looks could kill. When she turned her gaze to meet mine, I just gave her an innocent smile and raised my eyebrows as if to say, "Who, me?"

Kimberly stood up, brushed herself off, and went back to her seat. There was no more skirmishing for the next half hour.

Finally, the door opened and Mr. Clark came hurrying in. He crooked his finger, motioning us to follow him.

Both of us exchanged a nervous look, then we stood. Kimberly stepped back and let me pass through first. As soon as I walked through the door, I wondered if she had let me go first so she could stab me in the back.

But my imagination was running away with me. All she did was shut the door behind us.

"Sit," Mr. Clark ordered curtly.

We each took a seat in front of his desk.

Mr. Clark put on his glasses, studied the piece of paper before him, then put it down and took off his glasses. "The election results are in. And Ms. Wallace, you are the winner by a very wide margin.

Congratulations on your victory, and congratulations on the plan you devised. I'll be sending out letters to parents, the school board, and the participating merchants. If everyone responds quickly and favorably, we should be able to reinstate the privilege within the next two weeks."

"Thank you, Mr. Clark," I said softly.

Mr. Clark picked up his glasses and jabbed them in the air in Kimberly's direction. "As for you, young lady, I'm giving you another four Saturday detentions."

"But I already have—"

Mr. Clark didn't let her finish. "And you can count yourself fortunate that you are not suspended. Ms. Haver, we are delighted to have you back at Sweet Valley Middle School, but not to the extent that we would overlook a dishonest act of this magnitude. I do not know who assisted you in this effort, and I don't want to know. I am holding you and you alone responsible for your actions, and I suggest that you repeat this conversation to your friends so that in the future we will have no more unpleasant misunderstandings." He nodded his head at Kimberly. "You may go."

As soon as Kimberly had gone, Mr. Clark stood. I stood also, and he extended his hand. "Congratulations, Ms. Wallace. I commend your efforts and applaud your initiative. I'm sorry that you had to be the victim of such underhanded campaign schemes."

I smiled. "It's OK. But Mr. Clark?"

"Yes?"

"How did you know what Kimberly had done? I didn't tell, and none of my friends did."

Mr. Clark smiled. "I can't give away all my secrets, can I?"

On the way to lunch, I heard some footsteps behind me, and somebody draped something over my shoulders. I looked over and saw Evie, jogging along beside my elbow. What she had draped over my shoulders was my Unicorn jacket. "Isn't it great. Isn't it fantastic!" She was wearing her jacket, too. "Just think, we thought we had lost everything. But we won. *We won!*"

"Wait up!"

Maria and Elizabeth came running from the bank of lockers behind us. They were wearing their Unicorn jackets, too.

"Hello, Ms. Student Council President," said Elizabeth with a grin.

Maria just gave me a hearty smack on the arm.

People were milling past us on their way to the cafeteria. Lots of them said "Congratulations" as they passed.

All of us had brought our lunches today, and we went straight to the Unicorner to join Mandy, who was sitting by herself. She looked slightly wary as we sat down. But nobody said anything about the election. It was just chitchat, as usual, until . . .

"We're here to settle up," said a voice behind me.

We all turned. Kimberly took off her jacket and thrust it toward me. I caught it just as Ellen, Lila, and Jessica took their jackets off and thrust them at Maria, Evie, and Elizabeth.

"But I don't care how many jackets you guys have," Kimberly said with a sneer. "You'll never be real Unicorns."

I stood up as tall and straight as I could. "Well, P.S. We don't want to be Unicorns. At least I don't." With that, I thrust Kimberly's jacket into her arms, pulled mine off, and threw it right at her so that it covered her head.

"P.P.S.," Maria said, rising. "That goes for all of us."

Suddenly, Kimberly and her crowd were standing there loaded down with Unicorn jackets.

There was a choking sound at the end of the table. It was from Mandy. She was still wearing her jacket, but her face looked white and forlorn.

"This is it, Mandy," Kimberly said in a rough voice. "The Unicorn Club is splitting from the goody-goodies. Are you in? Or are you out?"

Mandy stood slowly. Her lips were trembling, and there were tears running down her cheeks. But when she spoke, her voice rang out loud and clear. "I, Mandy Miller, do hereby resign as both president *and a member* of the Unicorn Club."

Several people sucked in their breath in surprise, and Kimberly's face almost looked hurt.

Slowly, Mandy removed her jacket and then

walked over and politely handed it to Kimberly. "P.P.P.S. I'm the one who told Mr. Clark you stole the speech."

All the color in Kimberly's face drained away. Lila, Ellen, and Jessica looked shocked and demoralized.

Mandy picked up her lunch bag, dropped it into the wastebasket, and walked out of the cafeteria.

"I don't get it," Ellen said. "Is she resigning from them or us or what?"

"Shut up, Ellen," Kimberly barked.

"Well, is she?" Ellen persisted.

Kimberly didn't bother to answer. She just jerked her head in the opposite direction and Ellen, Lila, and Jessica followed.

"I'm as confused as Ellen," Elizabeth said after they were out of earshot. "Is she resigning from them or us?"

"I don't know," Maria said. "Who are we, anyway?"

"A club," Elizabeth said. "A club dedicated to bringing out the best in its members and not the worst."

"Well, we can't call ourselves the Goody-Goodies," Evie pointed out. "We might as well call ourselves the Dorks if we do that."

"OK," I said. "Let's come up with another name."

"How about . . . ?" Elizabeth shot a tentative glance around the table but didn't finish her sentence.

We all leaned eagerly forward. "How about what?" I asked.

"How about calling ourselves the Angels."

"Hmmmmmm." I liked the sound of it. And judging by the faces around the table, everybody else did, too.

"Mary," Maria said. "You don't by any chance want to trade your tuna fish for my salami?"

"I'd be happy to," I answered.

"You're an angel," Maria said with a grin.

I looked around the table again and smiled. "We're all Angels now."

## SIGN UP FOR THE
## SWEET VALLEY HIGH®
## FAN CLUB!

Hey, girls! Get all the gossip on Sweet
Valley High's® most popular teenagers
when you join our fantastic Fan Club!
As a member, you'll get all of this really
cool stuff:

- Membership Card with your own
  personal Fan Club ID number
- A Sweet Valley High® Secret
  Treasure Box
- Sweet Valley High® Stationery
- Official Fan Club Pencil (for secret
  note writing!)
- Three Bookmarks
- A "Members Only" Door Hanger
- Two Skeins of J. & P. Coats® Embroidery
  Floss with flower barrette instruction
  leaflet
- Two editions of *The Oracle* newsletter
- Plus exclusive Sweet Valley High®
  product offers, special savings,
  contests, and much more!

Be the first to find out what Jessica & Elizabeth Wakefield are up to by joining the
Sweet Valley High® Fan Club for the one-year membership fee of only $6.25 each
for U.S. residents, $8.25 for Canadian residents (U.S. currency). Includes shipping
& handling.

Send a check or money order (do not send cash) made payable to "Sweet Valley
High® Fan Club" along with this form to:

**SWEET VALLEY HIGH® FAN CLUB, BOX 3919-B, SCHAUMBURG, IL 60168-3919**

NAME _____
(Please print clearly)

ADDRESS _____

CITY_____ STATE _____ ZIP_____
(Required)

AGE _____ BIRTHDAY_____ /_____ /_____

Offer good while supplies last. Allow 6-8 weeks after check clearance for delivery. Addresses without ZIP
codes cannot be honored. Offer good in USA & Canada only. Void where prohibited by law.
©1993 by Francine Pascal                                                    LCI-1383-123